S.J. Wist

Infinity Dreamt Books

Published by Infinity Dreamt

Author's website: www.sjwist.com

ISBN: 978-0-9916914-3-2

ONE

Ten years ago...

"My very birth was the Prophecy that was to lead to the Caelestis' return to Aster and save Aragmoth himself. It would be my death that would curse it all back to the very beginning of hate between the immortal memories of caels. Memories that had not been healed by Time. Forgiveness, it would seem, is more of a mortal belief where life is too short to waste it on bitterness.

"We ruled the skies for two years after Cirrus pulled me to the surface of the Eternal Waters on the day of my Trial of Somn. Of his memory, I know I was dead for the twenty minutes that it took him to do so. Or at least, it felt like death when I woke up on another world. A world so much more advanced than ours. It felt like a Dream that I didn't want to wake from, but when I did, Cirrus was right there beside me just as he promised.

"I had surfaced from my Trial of Somn baptized in death, to bring death. The phelan of the Atrum's Army had begun to call Cirrus the White Death soon after that day, for wherever we went we brought devastation and a cold, suffocating death. We drove the griffin camps off of the Torian Continent and destroyed one Gate after the other, sending the phelan and griffins fleeing for their lives at every turn. Soon our mere presence was enough to send their armies crying into the hills.

"I became a monster of the skies, and in doing so I was now my father's most cherished son. No longer was I a useless child. I was the Prince reigning in a new era for our kind with the horrendously deformed and ugly shift of a dragon form that had been given to me. The era that would see the whole world die by our blades and wings of winter.

"For every life that we took, I could feel a part of my soul die. If Cirrus had let me give up, I might have died within that first year. But in continuing to live and kill, I didn't care what glory it brought my father's name or mine. I only did it to see her on Earth in what time I could steal to Dreamwalk. Cirrus seemed to define his own existence by the number of lives he was able to snuff out. If my sacrifice brought them purpose, I would feel happiness from them.

"The more I fought the longer I was able to sleep and

fall away from my reality of nightmares into the world of Dreams where she would always be there waiting for me. Humans who were victims to despair were fragile, brittle creatures. I could only bring her words to keep her from shattering so I could have more time to find a way to reach her. If I had learned of how to stay on her world, I could have protected her forever.

"I felt trapped on Aster, like a mer damned to roam the sea floor despite the light and endless free air well above its eyes. I would always wake up here. I could not die, for death would not allow me to.

"Then I found a way, by the claws of a thousand plumas that were able to cut me free from my shift. Now Daath needed to find a way to free me from Aragmoth so I would be his slave forever. The Atrum had their own Prophecy; that the Cael Daath would return to Aster and lead them in their conquest of Aster and Earth alike. But it would be a conquest fuelled by Daath's need for revenge.

"Now that I've finally broken free of the dark prison I was in, I feel as if everything has gone on without me, leaving only fragments of a nightmare in place of the time I have lost. Cirrus and Sybl were waiting for me, and now both of their Fates have taken the place of my own. I was too late to save them.

"They could have destroyed me or left me to my nightmare forever. Friends, it would seem, are something that defies the simplicity of life, death and reasoning."

There is a Heaven for each of us, and you have both left me so very alone in yours. Nafury looked at his mother's grave, and then at Sybl's and Cirrus' that lay next to it. He felt lost without anything or anyone to guide him to where he should go next.

"If you could save the world by saving one person, wouldn't it be worth it to try?"

Nafury stood up and looked back. When he didn't see anyone, he held his breath and closed his eyes. Then he opened them again into a trance.

Sybl stood there, smiling as she waved her hand playfully at him. "Cirrus was right, you are really good with Threads. Even when you aren't possessed by an evil force and trying to take over the world."

"I'm sorry," he said, not knowing what else he could say.

She shook her head. "It's already forgotten. Soon everyone else will forget and move on as well."

"What am I to do now without you both?"

"You have lots of wishes left in you, you just have to remember the better ones. I left you one of my own as well to give you a head start." She spun around to leave, but then turned back to face him again. "Oh, and do me and Cirrus a favour—don't drop it."

Nafury blinked, and in the moment that it took him to do so, she had vanished from sight with his trance. *Drop it?*

He walked out onto the ledge of the cave in the Bedlam Waterway as he tried to figure out the riddle. *Prophecy...* He remembered how Cirrus had teased him about dropping the 'Prophecy' that was Sybl before Daath brought her to Aster. She could only mean something that he could hold. Maybe even someone.

"You look as if you just saw a ghost," Cecil said, landing next to him on the ledge.

"I did," Nafury replied.

"What did it say?" the blue dragon asked curiously, as Nafury had always had Serena's ability as a Seer.

"I think there's another Fay."

TWO

Nafury didn't know why he had come out here. Maybe because for so long, this place was the edge of the world. The Ice Fields were miles and miles of freezing cold. The field he stood on separated the chimeras and Awls' domain from the Atrum's. One of the Great Dragon's wings formed the Efereal Mountains. The other formed the Dragon Caverns on the Torian Continent, where he was no longer welcome.

The bitter-cold winds that came from the mountain passed through his white cloak. It was not enough to turn the Fallen Prince's eyes from the sky. The atmosphere's pinkish-purple light overhead looked colder than here. For Nafury, the light was colder than all the snow on the desolate field. It was a constant reminder of his past and of his sister. His sister who was sacrificed so that life could defrost on Aster and not freeze to death.

He looked at the snow before him where the body of an aspiring phelan shifter lay. The drifting snow had covered most of his frozen corpse now, but the blood wasn't hidden by it. The body's right arm and left leg were torn off and thrown some meters away. This was where the phelan came to challenge their shifts. The massive wolf-like monster spirits would merge with them if they survived. If they failed to take down the spirit during their Trial, they died. Their body would rot and be forgotten where it fell.

From what Nafury had heard from within the taverns he drifted in and out of, it had been different once. Before the Aeger, the Trial of Somn was not so hard to survive. Had this teenager been born before the Aeger, he would have tackled a snow serpent or two, instead. The offering would have been given to his future shift. Now, the serpents were one of the many species on Aster that were extinct. The remaining spirits had resorted to killing the living, instead of protecting them like they were created to do.

He didn't know what the success rate was compared to a dragon's chances in their own Trials. Yet it was clear that the balance of life and death was still off on Aster.

Nafury was looking for his own death, but it

continued to run away from him. Only on the verge of it could he see her for a moment. The same eyes they shared in this life as brother and sister, reflecting back at him. He was alive and she was dead, yet her eyes showed no sadness. No hate of him. She only showed him pity for how much regret he drowned himself in. It was no use trying to swim for air or despair deeper, for she held him right where he was. So he accepted it as his punishment; his own limbo between being alive and the death that he so longed for.

On more than one occasion he had seen Cirrus in his nightmares as well, though it was hard to read his eyes. His face was always the solid, frozen state that matched the dragon form he once had. Nafury still remembered his best friend trying to kill him. Nafury's corrupted shift had killed Sybl, and now both her and Cirrus were dead because of him. He concluded that there were no bonds of friendship left between them before his death. It could be the only reason he saw him in his waking and sleeping nightmares at all.

Nafury took off his gold-plated helmet and scanned the barren landscape of ice with his eyes and psi. There was nothing to see and no thoughts of another for miles. He looked back at the gold that decorated his helmet. This was all he had left of a life he once knew, a life where he was once the Prince of Toria. That privileged life was gone. A small smile snuck onto his face.

He remembered how Cirrus had teased him over this helmet. To his friend Nafury supposedly looked more like he had a demon on his head than a dragon's horns. If only he could see Cirrus again to tell him how he had been so inadvertently right all along.

This was the only thing the Packs that answered to Kenshe hadn't taken from him yet, and his armor. Maybe they thought that the Threads of the gold metal were tainted with evil still. Realistically they were, for gold could preserve the memories of others in it. This helmet held his lifetime of sad, beautiful, and youthful memories. That was before he let his shift, Daath, overtake him. Perhaps that was why the phelan didn't want it. They seemed more content to believe him as nothing more than a monster. A monster rather than the human he was.

Something brushed past his thoughts. Nafury looked up and across the snowy desert as it swirled aimlessly around in the wind. It had about as much direction as he did now; absolutely none.

Nafury turned his head when his dark sapphire eyes caught a cloud of snow and antlers in the distance. It wasn't a phelan shifter out here today, but what looked like a stag.

'UNHOLY ONE.'

Nafury was completely focused on the cloud now as the name hit him like a sharp knife in the back. This wasn't just some stag, but an Awl as only they could take on a human form aside from the shifters, and use psi as well. While the world battled it out with their own shifts, the chimeras stayed quietly hidden. Only this one was being chased further from the safety of its mountain by one of Kenshe's Packs.

His common sense told him to stay out of this as it wasn't any of his business. He didn't know how much luck he had left with his avoiding of a direct confrontation with them. Yet this Awl was one of the few creatures on the planet who remembered him while he was Daath.

Nafury turned around with his choice to stay out of it. Blocking his leave, Sial stood silently watching him. The shaggy brown, horse-like creature carried the Threadless festra on its forehead. It was a weapon that once belonged to his sister. It was a masterless weapon that only he could wield now, as the Caelestis wasn't alive anymore to use it. She had freed the True he had bond to it in a previous life, so it was only a relic now.

"We must help Xirel."

"You mean that stag?"

"Yes, he is my brother."

Nafury pondered Sial's words for a moment. He remembered that many of the older chimeras were born of Nephena, the Mother of all Chimeras. Like their mother, they could be a mix of just about any animal. The kyrie claimed that the stag was his brother, which was possible. "Sorry, but I'm not going anywhere near that Pack."

"They will not harm you."

I'm not interested in trying my luck.

"They will not harm you. I cannot fight them alone," the kyrie insisted, and nudged Nafury with his muzzle.

Sial had never asked him for anything before. Nor had he ever spoken more than a few words. He ultimately couldn't say no as he owed the creature for saving his life on several occasions.

Nafury looked back as Xirel continued to run desperately towards them. He grabbed Sial's horn and pulled himself up onto his back. The kyrie wasted no time bursting into a run on an intercept course with the stag and Pack.

Sial was faster than any kyrie or chimera on Aster, and for a good reason. He was the kyrie that had protected the Caelestis' weapon for over three hundred years. Nothing alive could catch Sial, not even Nafury when he was possessed by the Awl demon, Daath. Now all he had left of his sister was her weapon that Sial carried as his horn. That and the gold fairy pendant on his neck that matched the one she took with her into death.

They caught up to the stag and Sial ducked as the stag chimera leaped over them. Before Nafury could so much as think of what to do next, he had his sword in hand. It found an immediate target across the chest of the phelan that had been directly behind the chimera.

Sial sprung back to his feet with an unnatural grace for his size, and spun around. The entire Pack stopped the chase to focus on them. Well, almost the entire Pack, as Feryl was still trying to heal the deep cut across his chest. It was a bitch to be wounded as an estus-creature these days. Yet it was fitting as the phelan were the first to lose the light of aeri energy from their souls after Sybl's death.

Nafury jumped down from Sial's back. He held his blood-covered long sword at the ready as the Pack circled him.

'Before I bite your useless head off, I'd like to know exactly what the hell you think you're doing?' Feryl unshifted into his human-like appearance in a fury of grey mist. He held the bleeding wound on his chest that mirrored the one he had suffered in his phelan form.

You're hunting Xirel like some stag, and I want to know why. Has Kenshe officially declared war against the whole world?

Feryl gave him the dumbest look Nafury had ever seen on his normally twisted face. The black-and-white-haired shifter looked at the stumbling stag. Xirel chose to stay beside Sial who shielded him from any straying teeth. Then he looked back at Nafury. *'That's not a chimera, you blatant idiot. Look at it! Is it speaking? Thinking past its survival? No. Xirel was strong enough to take out an Earth Sentry, and that deer over there is nothing close.'*

Suddenly doubt began to fill Nafury as he looked at the supposed Xirel. The stag collapsed from blood loss against the snow. Still, Sial refused to let up his guard. "The Caelestis' kyrie believes he is Xirel, so that's exactly who he is."

Feryl's stupid look remained only a moment longer, before he burst out into laughter. The other four of the Pack followed suit. "The Caelestis is DEAD. Or did you forget you killed her already? So as far as I'm concerned, she has no Ancient anymore or any need for one."

Sial, say something to them! Nafury shouted at the kyrie's psi. Sial responded by saying and thinking nothing to the Pack. It was as if he suddenly lost his psi and ability to speak as well, or just wasn't heard.

The former Prince was counting his heartbeats now as the Pack began to negotiate which of them would kill Sial and which would kill Xirel. Time was running out faster than he could think of a way to get out of this mess.

"Has your dead Goddess proclaimed that we are to stop eating meat?" Feryl asked him, and the Pack laughed again.

With the situation precariously in pause, Nafury took a moment to look where the stag lay on his side. He was dying and Nafury's limited aeri without a shift of his own would likely not be enough to save its life. He reached out his psi to Xirel then, and the chimera's mind connected with his first.

'Fay...must reach her before it's too late.'

Nafury stopped breathing, allowing only his mind to inhale all of Xirel's thoughts. He grasped for everything the stag had just said, ignoring the pain from the creature that he had also taken in. *Where is she?*

'Here.' Then Xirel closed his purple eyes and passed out.

Nafury lowered his sword, before remembering that he had to breathe again. He didn't get the chance to when a fist went for his face with enough force to drop him to the ground.

"Worthless sack of garbage you are," Feryl said as he spat a glob of blood next to Nafury's face. "If you didn't have so much sickening sentimental value to the Boss, you would already be dead."

Nafury watched as Feryl went to pick up his helmet from where it had fallen. "The gold on this should be enough to make up for the scar you gave me."

"Don't take that!" Nafury pleaded.

"Oh we're taking it, and your kyrie too." On Feryl's words, the Pack began to snap at Sial who continued to guard Xirel's body.

Sial lowered his horn defensively, refusing to give up.

Run you stupid beast! They will kill you! Nafury shouted at the creature's mind.

Sial did no such thing. Nafury looked around them as the Animus Threads began to vibrate dangerously. But

Sial wasn't an Awl, at least he wasn't from what Nafury knew. He was a chimera who had amassed his intelligence and strength entirely by himself. There was no foreign spirit within him. His strength would prove real, as the ground lifted from under the phelan. Gravity reversed and set them all afloat. Then it exploded outward with the concentrated force of a tornado.

THREE

Kenshe had started his day off interestingly enough. First, the attack on the Efereal Mountains which failed as they did not kill all the traitors. Next, his entire Pack being hurled near death, supposedly by a kyrie. Kas' former kyrie for that matter. Now, the leader of the traitor Awls awaited him as he pulled a stool over and sat down in front of Xirel. He had strung the Awl from the ceiling in the lower dungeons of the Atrum. It would only hold until the chimera regained his strength, assuming he survived that long.

There was no avoiding the worry he had that his Pack may have taken Xirel's treatment a bit too far. When they attacked the Efereal Mountains, their orders were to kill the stag Awl first. What no one expected was that the chimera leader had built a new Gate, and was on Earth at the time of the attack. By now, all of the Awl Tribes across the Continent would have heard of the attack. That, in turn, put the Atrum in the center of a whole lot of dangerous enemies.

What was supposed to be a simple plan was now a complete mess. On top of it all, they did not expect that the Deathmare would show up. It effectively blew apart what ever might be salvageable of the situation. The Caelestis' kyrie had been a laughed-at fairy tale with the secret power it was rumoured to have. Kenshe wasn't laughing now.

The Awl had remained a dozen steps ahead of him, but this was where it would end. Xirel was still bleeding from a wound to his side, yet he refused to let any of their healers' aeri energy heal him. The griffin metal that held him prevented him from using his own energy.

"You pray for all the wrong things...Kenshe," Xirel said as he locked his purple eyes on the Atrum Lord.

"And I suppose she answers your prayers?" Kenshe replied.

"The Caelestis speaks to me all the time. Even now, I can feel the gentle breeze of her psi...reaching out in concern for me. She will return from the realm of death. If you harm me further, then that will be the end of the Atrum and all concerning it, including you," Xirel warned.

"If you hadn't left the Atrum's Order, then none of this would have happened to begin with," Kenshe replied.

"I do not answer to you. None of my chimera ever will trust your kind again. I had hoped that Sybl's memory might be enough to unite us, but you have forgotten her. Therefore, the peace between our kind has also been forgotten. "

"Your chimera Awls will not be a problem once you are dead. Though, I am curious to just what you were looking for on Earth to have left them so vulnerable?"

"You are a fool, Kenshe. Once you might have been a great leader, but you have become corrupt. The blood of Solar that runs in your veins from your dragon mother has betrayed you. Why I was on Earth is none of your concern, for I have nothing more to say to you." Xirel's eyes flared a bright purple for a moment before fading.

Kenshe got to his feet and started to leave. "Then die for all I care."

Xirel had drifted off for an unknown amount of time when a small voice woke him. Only after opening his eyes did he realized that the gentle voice had not come from his head, but from in front of him. "You should not be here — it is too dangerous."

"It's my fault that you're here," the small voice replied.

"You have not received any training with your powers. You need to get out of here before anyone sees you."

"And go where?" the girl asked as she pulled over the stool and stood on it to try her luck with the shackles that hung him up. "Where are the keys?"

Xirel only sighed and dropped his head as Ubi looked in the direction that the phelan shifter had left in.

"I'm not leaving here without you," the girl insisted and pulled her black hood back over her head. With a quick look back, she followed after the Atrum Lord.

Xirel pulled harder at his shackles, cursing the fact that they were made from griffin metal. He closed his eyes tight as he tried to think of how to save her, chorused by prayers to Sybl for a miracle.

FOUR

Nafury didn't know how long he had been out for when he opened his eyes. It could have only been a while, as he had been dragged into a cell. The cold, dark energy that surrounded him meant that he could only be in the Atrum's dungeon.

"Took you long enough to wake up." The voice registered familiar before the dark figure standing in front of his cell did.

"Here I was truly starting to believe that we were becoming friends," Nafury replied.

Kenshe grabbed one of the cell bars. "You took everything from me, yet I went on believing that there was a reason somewhere to keep you alive. It would seem that you are incurably cursed with how you always manage to be in the wrong place at the wrong time. I'm out of patience."

"Everything to you?" Nafury laughed at the idea of his sister holding a phelan shifter equally in such high regard. Let alone a kid as messed up as the current Atrum Lord.

"You know nothing," Kenshe said bitterly as his eyes glowed momentarily red.

Nafury lifted his hands in mock surrender to the argument. "Seeing as you haven't already killed me, I can only guess that I'm still important to you. No one has to know of the assassin squad you let loose on the Efereal Mountains. Besides, there are few who would hear any of my words at all."

"The chimeras and Awls were proving too complicated to reason with," Kenshe explained. He crouched down before Nafury's cell to get a better look at him. "I was going to keep you alive for the sake of Sybl's sacrifice, but you have gone out of your way this time to find that death you seek. Tomorrow, you and Xirel will be executed for treason."

Nafury rested his head against the back of his cell and laughed. "Treason? Don't I have to pledge allegiance to you first for that to happen? Come on, Kenshe. That is so unfair. We were supposed to die with a mortal grip on each other's throats as we fell straight into Hell. Now you're going to what? Behead me? How uncivilized. My sister is not going to be happy about any of it."

Kenshe stood up and didn't answer him.

"But if Sybl wants my soul next to hers now, then I'm

not going to fight to live. You just really need to tell me what in all the Hells she ever saw in you."

"If she doesn't like who I've become to hold Kas' legacy together, she is welcome to take it up with me personally."

"How about I make this personal between us?" a voice said from down the hall.

Kenshe looked at the young teenage ayame. "What are you doing down here?"

"You hurt Xirel, and now I'm going to make you pay for it!"

Kenshe wasn't phased, and he didn't bother to reach for his blade.

Nafury got to his feet and looked from the other side of the bars to his little rescuer. There was something about her that she was using a great deal of her concentration to keep hidden.

"I have not called for you. Leave," Kenshe ordered.

"How dare you speak to me like I'm one of your dogs!" the voice hissed back and bright blue eyes replaced the red glow as the girl's hood lifted. Her eyes focused on Kenshe's wolf-like shift that stood just a little ways behind him in its spirit form.

Kenshe's right hand was on the Threads around him to form a defence now. The blue glow of her eyes was uncanny. But she didn't attack him directly. Instead, his own shift came straight at him from behind with a mouthful of teeth that caught his shoulder and arm in a vice grip. Unable to fight back as he was, his shift dashed down the hall, carrying him as if he were a mere corpse.

Nafury was certain that he was the next to die.

The girl picked up the keys that had been dropped by Kenshe and looked at Nafury. Then she looked around his cell, likely looking for his spirit shift. "You don't have one, do you?"

"Your power..." was all that Nafury could say. "You are who Sybl was talking about—the other Fay."

The girl's blue eyes dimmed and returned to being red, as if by reflex to defend her identity. "Can you use aeri energy?"

"Yes, but these bars are griffin metal," Nafury stated as he eyed the keys in her hand.

"I need you to help me heal someone, and in return I will help you to escape," the girl said.

"Xirel," Nafury concluded, and watched as she unlocked his cell.

"Yes."

He followed the girl down the halls and up a set of stairs. They soon found Xirel strung up in chains in a larger cell like meat left in the freezer. "You weren't kidding," he said to the chimera Awl in regard to their newest Fay. Nafury caught him after the girl released the second shackle lock. The Awl was tall, but couldn't have weighed half of what he did. He channeled some of his aeri into Xirel's wounds. He started with the flesh that had been ripped away with phelan teeth at his side. Within moments the Awl began to come around.

"I never obtained much of a sense of humour..." Xirel confessed. "Ubi," he continued, looking at the girl.

"I'm okay. Right now we need to get you out of here," she replied.

"Why would you need a sense of humour?" Nafury thought aloud as he pulled Xirel's arm behind his neck to help keep him upright. Then they slowly started out of the dungeon.

"Because...this is the third time a human is rescuing me."

Nafury looked the way they came as several shouts and screams went out.

"I've turned their shifts on them. We need to use the commotion to escape," the young woman said.

Nafury looked at Ubi, taking note that Xirel said that it was the third time.

Ubi's eyes remained red. She fluttered around Xirel, as if trying to generate enough wind to propel him back to his own feet. "Is he going to be okay?"

"He's peachy. But the whole Atrum is likely to come down on us now," Nafury said.

They passed like silent shadows as the phelan shifter guards battled it out with their own shifts in the halls. None of them seemed to have the slightest idea to just what was going on.

Kenshe's secret assassination plan was still a secret. It was fortunate for them, for none of the soldiers looked long at them or saw three prisoners making an exit. They made no eye contact with any one, until they were well out of the black castle, through Ubi's means of entry.

Sial met them not far from the courtyard. Nafury helped the girl onto his back, and pulled himself up behind her. Xirel staggered a moment, but soon managed to shift into his white stag form. Giving the stag only a moment to count the legs under him, they hastily made their way for the trees.

FIVE

Nafury opened his eyes and glanced around the rubble they sat amongst. It was all that was left of the Sanctus now. A part of him regretted not seeing the Temple in its glory before the Phoenix burned it to the ground.

"You humans sleep far too much."

Nafury looked across from him, where Xirel held the sleeping girl in his arms. Nafury's once-white, now-battered cloak covered her. She seemed perfectly content to make the chimera Awl into her personal pillow. He checked that the fairy pendant on his neck was still there, and let out a breath of relief as his cloak was all that she took. "She's like Sybl, isn't she?"

Xirel pulled some of the almost-black hair from Ubi's face and studied her closer. "She looks just like Kas, but she has her mother's character."

So this was Xirel, the chimera's leader. He would

never have guessed such a frail looking Awl to be capable of achieving much. His long white hair, purple eyes, and bone-thin physique left a lot of questions to how he led anything.

"How insulting of you. Your sister thought that I was truly beautiful," Xirel replied nonchalantly to Nafury's thoughts. He stared at him now with purple eyes that were hard to read. "It would seem that the memories you retained after Daath's exorcism are limited."

"I try to not think about how I nearly destroyed two realms too often. Has a rather depriving affect on my mood," Nafury replied, trying to not let it get to him.

"And so it should. I would have seen to it myself that you were killed for what you did. Sybl was irreplaceable, both as a Fay and who she was."

"It wasn't my choice to stay alive, it was hers," Nafury replied, trying to keep his tone neutral. An Awl was not something he could fight and hope to live. He looked at Ubi for a change of subject. "This Fay can only be her daughter. But how?"

"Her soul is of the Fay who was born to Erebus and Asil on the first Aster. As such, she is also Sybl's daughter," Xirel explained, his tone once again neutral.

"If this is true, then why are we finding her now? She must be at least fifteen."

"Her past is a tragic and complicated one."

Nafury rubbed his cold arms as he gave a quick look

to the Threads around them, sensing for any danger. "She was reincarnated on Earth?"

"Indeed. But she has been made fragile and hateful. Earth's Sentries have slaughtered her countless times over the millennium. Everyday a bit more of her dies as she remembers the injustice done to her."

Nafury looked at Xirel. "Kas supposedly had all his memories of his life on the first Aster as Erebus. Why didn't he do something about that?"

"Because Kas was the one who banished her there," Xirel answered.

"Why would he do that? Who could do that for that matter?"

"Her power is very dangerous, and while she is a human now, I cannot speak for how she may have been as a complete Fay. I do know, however, that Kas never did anything without carefully calculating its repercussions. He was the exact opposite of his soultwin in that respect."

"Does she know who I am?" Nafury asked and finished with a gulp.

"Yes, I told her while you were asleep."

"Does she blame me for what happened?"

"No. I told her that you were possessed and Sybl saved you. That's all I told her of you," Xirel replied.

Nafury relaxed a little. The rest of the story could wait, for now. Or forever.

"She believed that Sybl purposely left her alone and

motherless. Only, it wasn't your sister's fault. Kas took the memories of their daughter into death with him. It was why he never became close with Sybl, lest that memory return to her."

"But why would he do something like that? This is their daughter we're talking about!"

"Erebus was the one to cast out Ubi from the first Aster and send her to Earth. She was an abomination; a threat to the stability of the planet and considered a monster. As you have already seen, she can bend shifts to her will. I made the mistake of touching her when I found her on Earth. Without warning and entirely by reflex, she ripped my Awl self right out of my shift. If I didn't look so horrifying in that state she might have killed me right there. Fortunately, she remembered me from her previous incarnation, when I was still a Sentry. So I got a hold of myself again and grabbed her quick and brought her back through the Gate. But Kenshe's army was waiting when we returned and we were separated. She utilized one of the True to reach the Atrum and rescue us."

A howl went out from the True in the distance. Nafury wondered if they could hear this far. "If she wasn't right there, I wouldn't believe any of it." He focused back on Xirel's unreadable eyes. "How do you know so much?"

"Awls were once Sentry on Earth. I once watched Hino kill one of her previous incarnations before my very eyes. It was on that day that I made the choice to come to

Aster. Asteria once granted you and the other Three Generals a soul and a place on her world. Similarly, the Great Dragon allowed me to live in a body that the Chimera Mother had killed in her fury. The will of the Caelestis within the Great Dragon makes Him merciful."

"Next to your sickly appearance, what was your flaw?" Nafury asked, curious. He remembered bits and pieces of the Last War when he was Damek. The chimeras had retaliated for being slaughtered for their imperfections and the Feharin had won the War, but lost their Golden City and the Third Continent. More importantly, they had lost Sybl when she was Asil.

Sadness darkened Xirel's purple eyes and he didn't answer him. Instead, he looked at Ubi. "Time is against us. We only have until all her memories return to save her, and there is another problem as well."

"Like the entire Suzerain Continent now hunting us down?" Nafury said.

"Your adopted father is still alive. In saving Ubi, I also unavoidably opened the Gate for his return here. He is going to come for her."

"Oh just great," Nafury replied. "Of all the damn problems we have to deal with as it is, that bastard has to still be alive." He looked at Ubi as she slightly tilted her head their way. She was likely listening in on their conversation while pretending to be asleep.

"Mind your words, Fallen Prince, for Simera has been

keeping her safe until I found her. He will come for her. If she falls into his hands on Aster, he will use her to burn the Suzerain Continent to the ground."

"Then let him, why should I care if he does? Kenshe would have seen us killed in a cold corner of his spire. Then he would have dumped our bodies amongst a heap of garbage."

"Yes, but with Ubi things have changed. Kenshe will have likely guessed by now who he was attacked by. Then there is the matter where I do not believe that the Simera I fought was the same dragon king who left Aster," Xirel said.

"What do you mean?"

"He seemed different. If not, out of touch with himself. If something has overcome Simera, you would likely spot it much easier than myself."

"So we can't run to Toria, and we can't stay here or at the Efereal Mountains. Just where are we to go?" Nafury asked.

Xirel looked to Ubi as she sat up and let out a huge yawn.

"All right, I'll ask her," Nafury said and looked at her. "Where are we going, Princess?"

"I'm not a princess," she replied. "So spare me the little girl talk."

The side of Nafury's mouth twitched at her razor-edge response. He gathered up his cloak from the snow to momentarily disengage himself from the war spark before him. Then he looked towards the trees on sensing someone watching them.

"Kenshe's Pack is back, which means they are here to finish what they started," Xirel said as he got to his feet.

Nafury caught sight of the slender wolf-cat like form of the ayame. It was now their biggest problem, as a Call from her could send the Pack into an unstoppable killing frenzy. "I don't suppose you can take her on?"

Xirel didn't answer, as his fingers moved to defensively organize the Threads around them.

Nafury unsheathed his blade and looked at Ubi who was already a step ahead and flustering the phelans.

"Don't move," Xirel instructed, and lifted his hand to grab and pull down on the invisible Thread around them.

A scream of pain went out, then the furious barks and howls of the Pack as they rushed towards them.

Xirel lifted his hand again, and made a swift motion to the side. The remaining four phelan of the Pack collapsed against the snow like puppets.

"You killed the ayame," Nafury said more matter-of-factly than as a question.

Xirel lowered his hand, as his face finally became readable. It had become laden with fear. "I did not deal her a lethal blow..."

Nafury froze in turn when the air around them became an uneasy stillness. It was eerily familiar. When the shadow of a dragon blocked out the light of the Sylvan Aur on them, it became clear that they weren't the only Thread puppeteers here.

SIX

No one moved except Xirel. The Awl only slightly twitched his fingers as Simera landed some meters from them. The dragon darkened the snow around it with a shadow of fear that stretched well beyond his size.

Nafury tried to reach out his psi to Simera, but it was as if he was calling someone who was far away. "I think you're right—that's not the Simera I remember, either."

Xirel slowly nodded as his entire focus remained on the Black Death before them. It wasn't often that dragons faced off against Awls, but it almost always ended badly. They usually ended up killing each other.

Nafury looked to his feet as he could feel Simera's power swell where he stood.

"When he strikes, take Ubi and run," Xirel whispered without looking at Nafury.

"What about you?" Nafury asked in concern.

"She's more important than either of us," Xirel said. His hand began to slowly rise to match the growing dark power under them.

Simera's light blue eyes glowed brighter. He was not tolerating their small movements.

Nafury had less than a heartbeat to react when Simera unleashed his power. The black dragon sent his mastery rushing towards them from the ground as a geyser of estus energy. It coated Nafury like a thick oil, before pulling him down to the ground.

Xirel was caught as well, but managed to snap enough Threads to free Nafury and Ubi from the black ooze. Then he cut another Thread with his nails which disabled Simera's front leg.

Nafury grabbed Ubi and made a run for it through the ruins of the Sanctus. He hoped against hope to cut the line of sight that made the dragon's power against them possible.

Ubi tried to keep up, but tripped over the rubble and landed hard on her hands and knees with a cry.

Nafury tried to get her back on her feet, but the Threads to his lungs were caught and pulled taught. He gasped for air, before falling to his own knees as he couldn't breathe. Seeing the fear in Ubi's eyes he forced himself to focus on his remaining air, not struggle the last of it out. He looked up as Simera landed on a wayward pillar overhead and looked down at them.

"Give me the Fay and I will grant you a swift death." Simera let out a warning growl.

Not going to happen. I won't let you turn her into the monster you made me into! Nafury shouted back at the dragon's psi.

"She is already just that! You do not understand the destructive power that you would protect so blindly!" Simera replied.

Nafury made a desperate gasp again, as Ubi tried to take control of Simera's shift. Blood dripped from her nose as she strained to make the dragon spirit listen. Just as Simera descended on them, she gained control of him and forced Simera from his dragon shift.

The dragon king let out a cry of pain, as the black mist dissipated and left him in his human-like appearance. His shift, a dark mauve spirit of a dragon, coiled and uncoiled its body in an attempt to break free of Ubi's control over it.

"Nafury!" Ubi cried to him, but he wasn't moving anymore. She looked at Simera who was quickly coming around and cried out for help, even as it seemed like there no one left to help.

The ruins began to shake, and Ubi dared to look down through the broken ceiling she stood on. Light blue eyes from a white figure looked back at her from the darkness.

The creature drew closer, and all at once the rubble exploded from under her. It effortlessly threw them all into the air. The white dragon caught Nafury first, pulling him into its shift. Then it caught her before she could hit the floor of the lower ruins. The last thing she heard was the white dragon's infuriated cry of vengeance. Her last sight of Simera was blinded with blood.

SEVEN

Simera's memories of Nafury's mother, Serena, were beautiful. The King of Dragons had selflessly given her everything and asked for nothing. The sad truth of it all was that he never loved her past friendship and his need to control her. It was a cold, lingering sadness that now took over Nafury's heart. He continued to watch the dragoon's memories play out in random before his eyes. The spirit that had hold of Nafury now burned hotter and hotter with hate at each image he saw. Finally, the heat became so overwhelming that it blinded his soul from seeing anything more.

'She was never destined for me,' Simera's voice said in the back of his mind, before it faded entirely.

Nafury opened his eyes to find himself hovering just out of reach of the Efereal Mountain. Its strong winds momentarily threatened to throw his balance off entirely. He was flying, and he didn't have the slightest idea how or why. He darted his gaze in all directions, before remembering enough about how to be a dragon and descended to land.

He wore a dragon form as white as the snow under him when he knew he should have been dead. He remembered how to unshift, and took on his human appearance again. The white mist dispersed around him, merging with the snow flurries. He expected to see his newest dragon shift beside him, but instead there stood the ghostly image of Alexia. He had only seen memories of her from others. She was supposed to have died long before he was born, giving birth to Cirrus. But she was an Awl, and he had heard that she had nearly forced Cirrus to kill Sybl at one point, and was imprisoned by Gei for it. She was beautiful, if only in a cold, defiant sort of way. Her blond hair fell around her feet, and her light blue eyes flashed unpredictably. She wore a simple white dress that looked like a design Earth might have made. "Alexia?"

She didn't answer, and he looked to his feet where Ubi had been set down asleep in the snow. Its coldness was enough to wake her, and she sat up momentarily before jumping to her feet from the sting of it.

"Nafury? Oh thank heavens—I thought you were dead!" she said in a panic and hugged him.

He returned the hug with his own and let out a breath

of relief. "Let's not do that again."

She nodded and pulled away, wiping some of the tears from her eyes. Ubi took a moment to acknowledge the woman spirit, before looking around for Xirel. "Where's Xirel?"

Nafury closed his eyes for a moment, trying to catch a Thread that might lead to Xirel. He found one, though it was faint. "He limping, again. But he's on his way here."

"Phew," Ubi said and focused back on Alexia. The two of them seemed to have a silent battle of wills before Ubi gave up. "Your shift is weird."

Alexia replied first with a sly smile. "I was momentarily worried that I would go from prisoner to your puppet. It would appear that you're strong, Fay, but still far from your true potential."

"How did you shift with me like that? I heard you were sealed away," Nafury said.

"I was, but the blood of that unholy one was enough to break me free."

At the mentioning of blood, Ubi quickly wiped the dried blood from her face.

"Unholy, eh?" Nafury said, unconvinced. He watched Ubi plant a handful of snow on her face to help her blood removal efforts. "I think you mean 'unruly.'"

"I'm glad to see that you haven't lost your sense of humour, Damek," Alexia said.

The way she said his previous incarnation's name sent

a chill down his spine. "I don't go by that name anymore," Nafury replied, instantly agitated.

"You are Damek and you will always be Damek. How else would you still be alive on a Continent of phelan had you not created them? Why else would you care about them at all?" Alexia continued.

"You're crazier than I've seen in the memories of my pendant. Just what do you want? Revenge? Just what did you do with Simera?"

"We will never have to worry about Simera again. And no, you did not kill Cirrus. Your sister and her foolish actions led to his death."

"My sister is the one who saved two worlds! How dare you!"

Alexia laughed as she changed into her dragon form. He was given a full view of her teeth now that looked physical enough to bite him in half if she chose to. "A monster calling me a monster. It must be true then. But unlike you, I am no fool. I know what is coming with that Fay here, and it will not be a swift death like the Aeger, but a long and treacherous war."

"With who? The dragons?" Nafury asked.

"The dragons are all puppets like Simera returned as. They are not a concern, for their strings are just as easily cut. Eventually, however, only the fingers and hand of their manipulator will remain."

"And who is that?" Ubi asked, having gotten all the

blood off of her face.

"I don't know. The Threads are tangled in such a way to hide the puppeteer well. They will make a mistake though, in time. That's when we must strike."

"I'm not teaming up with you," Nafury retorted, then looked to where Sial waited in the direction of the Efereal Mountains. He watched as Ubi went over to the kyrie to look him over.

"Is it because I tried to kill your sister where you succeeded? Will you not so much as ask me why?" Alexia said with an innocent tone.

"Fine, why?" Nafury asked bitterly.

"Because her mother stole you from Earth and the other Three Generals. You may have forgotten, but I have not forgotten that you were once mine."

"We left by choice because we were tired of being slaves," Nafury replied.

A large smile spread across Alexia's face, making her dragon form even more terrifying. "So you do remember. We were not slaves, Damek, we were gods. You abandoned that existence for the love of a Sylph that you will never have again. Even now you blindside the needs of others for the sake of your own. We were the same then, and we are the same now."

"No, we are not." Nafury turned to leave.

"You cannot protect Ubi as you are now, Damek. If Kenshe doesn't kill you, the other dragons will have their vengeance. It is only a matter of time before the news of Simera's death reaches them."

"If it is my time to join my sister in death, then so be it!" Nafury snapped at her. "I will not make the mistake of surrendering my soul to a monster ever again."

"Then it will be Ubi who becomes the monster in your place. What Simera said is true. Soon she will remember everything and you will not be strong enough to pull her from the darkness."

Nafury stopped walking, and turned his eyes from Sial to the frozen ground. "And what guarantee would I have that you don't try and kill Ubi yourself?"

"I have no quarrel with her. Sybl was all that was left of Asteria and my need for revenge has died with them both. Ubi may be the daughter of your sister's previous incarnation, but she is no Fay of light. There is more darkness in that child than in the heart of Aragmoth. If anything, I pity her. She could very well be the monster who ultimately tries to destroy you, and I'd rather see that not come to pass."

Nafury could feel Alexia's hate for Simera simmering down in his very blood. So his adoptive father was dead. Such was Alexia's extreme level of strength. There was nothing left for her to hate and kill. "Did you ever love your son, Cirrus?"

Alexia didn't reply immediately. "I died minutes after he was born. I was not given the chance to love him when

I was alive, but I loved him enough to keep him alive as long as I did as his shift."

"Only you don't die," Nafury added.

"Everything dies, Damek, except hate and love. The human form I had taken on Earth was killed. I returned to being what I am now. This Sentry form would have never worked well with Simera had I remained."

"So you became Cirrus' shift, forcing him to remain a dragon till he was a teen. Then your hateful attempt on Sybl's life forced Gei to separate you from him."

"I forced that on Gei, not the other way around. I knew that eventually Cirrus would be pitted against you in battle, and I had no intention to ever harm you. Moon was stronger for the task as well."

"So you chose to be potentially imprisoned for all eternity rather than harm me? I'm touched," Nafury mocked. He looked briefly at Ubi who was content to watch them debate it all out.

"Believe what you will. I don't waste time with lies," Alexia replied.

"So what do you get out of helping me?"

"I get what I always wanted," she replied.

"Which is?"

"You."

EIGHT

Nafury didn't believe the devastation that Kenshe had caused at the Efereal Mountains. The bodies of dozens of different animal variations of chimera lay strewn about. The smell of death was unbreathable while blood seemed to cover everything. The phelan left nothing that came within reach of their teeth alive.

Ubi knelt silently before the giant bear before her and looked to the spirit that hovered nearby. It was a casualty amongst dozens.

"Please do not despair, Ubi," Xirel said as he appeared behind them in the tunnel. "You did not do this."

Ubi sprung to her feet and charged Xirel so fast, he nearly fell over in his weakened state. "Xirel! Are you alright?"

The Awl smiled and set a gentle hand down on her head. "I will be fine. I told Nafury to run with you while I held Simera off, but flying worked as well." Xirel looked then at Nafury. "Assuming our latest and most unexpected help doesn't have anyone left on her list to kill?"

"I'll have to check it over twice later on," Nafury said and looked to where Alexia drifted along the wall. The Sentry pretended to be unfocused and passive.

"How could that bastard do something like this?" Ubi demanded to know. "Wasn't Kenshe close to my mother?" Her anger continued to build.

"Kenshe is no longer a child, and your mother only had so much time with him," Xirel replied.

"I should have had his own shift bite his head off," Ubi said as she patted a place on the bear's fur that was not splattered in blood. "He must have been magnificent when he was alive."

"He will be missed," Xirel said solemnly and looked away from them both.

"Kenshe has to pay for this," Ubi said as she gripped the bear's fur.

"No, Ubi. There has been enough bloodshed as it is, and I fear that there will be much more to come. Nafury has already killed what can only be one of our enemy's strongest assets, Simera. They no longer have you and they will think twice before striking out at us again," Xirel said.

Nafury could feel Xirel's need to protect Ubi from the lingering darkness in her mind. He wanted to do nothing less himself.

"I'm calling the True. I want every phelan shifter who spilled blood in this mountain tracked down and killed," Ubi said.

"Ubi!" Nafury said in concern.

"Will you try and stop me?" Ubi challenged. "I know you want them dead as well."

"Kenshe will get what's coming to him soon enough, but not like this," Nafury said.

"I saw how he humiliated you all these years. They constantly tormented you for what you had no control over to stop—I saw it all from Xirel's psi. How can you forgive him so easily? Geolan was one of the many who tried to surrender. Just like you, he didn't want to fight, but those bloodthirsty savages wouldn't let up!"

"Will killing the ones responsible make you feel better?" Nafury asked, trying to curb her temper. If she exploded on them now, he would lose her before he could fully grasp her trust. She was like dealing with an overheated Solar before the Last War.

"Yes," Ubi said without hesitation.

"Alright," Nafury said. "On the condition that you sleep on it. If you feel the same in the morning, I won't try and stop you. Heck, I will even help you."

Ubi took a moment to consider the deal before agreeing.

Xirel let out a silent sigh of relief and focused back on

the task at hand; regaining the lost sanity in his mountain.

Nafury had almost resorted to tying up and dragging Ubi to her given room that night. Pulling her away from Xirel had been one challenge. Getting her to go to sleep was a different one entirely. He got fed up watching her toss and turn and went over to her bedside. Nafury sat down next to her and she lay on her back and looked at him. They stared at one another in content silence for a while before she looked at his necklace.

Nafury removed his silver chain and its gold fairy, and began to wave it back and forth over her eyes. The only thing he hadn't tried yet was hypnotizing her to sleep.

"What is that?" Ubi asked. "It looks like a girl's."

"Once upon a time it belonged to Gei, who gave one to Serena and Alexia, before it was passed to me and Cirrus. From there, I gave mine to your mother when I Dreamwalked and saw her, and this one once belonged to my best friend. The gold retains all of the memories they shared. The Threads of gold can't be erased or changed."

Ubi reached out and took it from him, then looked it over. "How do I turn it on?"

"You have to be able to read Thread," Nafury said.

"Fortunately, your venison and myself are the second and third best teachers on Aster."

Ubi giggled as Xirel peeked in from the doorway on having been referred to as meat.

"Second to who?" Xirel challenged.

"To the wolf that had you hanging in his meat locker," Nafury replied. Surprisingly, Xirel didn't retort. Nafury would have to find the rare and elusive ego that the Awls were supposed to be such masters over. He took the necklace and fairy pendant back for a moment from Ubi before tying it around her neck. "There," he said and set it straight between her collar bones. "That way if Sybl's spirit reaches out to us, you will be able to feel her."

Ubi smiled, pleased with the gift. "Thank you."

"I wish I could give you the castle that was taken from me instead of a mere trinket of your mother's memory."

"Xirel said that it's like a giant white crystal—is that true?" Ubi asked, as her excitement continued to climb.

Nafury smiled and nodded. "You will see it, I promise."

"That should prove interesting," Xirel added. "Are you going to try and take it by force?"

"Toria is rightfully mine now. I killed Simera, and I am still his Queen's son."

"Alexia killed Simera," Xirel corrected. "And while you may be Serena's son, to the dragons, you killed your sister who was their Caelestis."

"While I was possessed," Nafury added.

"The dragons do not care about such details. Sybl was important to them as well."

Nafury let out a long sigh. "Kenshe hasn't announced his failed takeover of the Efereal Mountains to the masses yet, so the Order won't be looking for us. With some luck, we might be able to get to Toria and have our say on the matter before the rumours reach it."

"There is no luck, Fallen Prince, only Fate." Xirel left the room at that.

Nafury looked back at Ubi who was still wide awake.

"Is that true? That Fate rules Aster?" Ubi asked.

"I can't agree with everything the Great Dragon does, but most of the time it's for the better. The Animus Thread is his weaving. He holds all the strings, guards all the doors, rotates the Aurs, cycles all the living and dead, changes all the weather. Aster is very different from Earth. On Earth, everything is more chaotic."

"When I was in your shift, I saw a blond-haired man. He seemed important to you," Ubi said.

"He was my best friend, and Sybl's Bond in this life. Do you hate him for that?"

"No," Ubi said as she wiped her nose with the back of her hand. "It looked like he cared about you a lot. I think he would have been good to my mother, too."

Nafury pulled his white cloak off and wrapped it around her to add to the warmth of the blanket on her already. "He loved me, but to him, Sybl was everything. They both loved me enough to do the impossible and lose their lives to tear Daath from me. They should have just left me to Hino's wrath."

Ubi scanned his eyes, trying to understand the entirety of what he seemed unable to explain all in words. "It must be nice to have those who care about you that much. I wish I had family and friends like that."

"I don't know of your life on Earth, but you will never have to worry about that again. Xirel and I will always watch out for you."

"Promise?"

"Promise," Nafury said. "Besides, you're like a niece to me in this life which is rather neat. Family sticks together."

Ubi giggled as she pondered the idea of having an uncle. "I want to see more of your friend, Cirrus. If he was important to you, then I want him to be important to me as well. Maybe it will help draw my mom's spirit closer, if anything."

Nafury nodded and reached out a hand to touch her face. He closed his eyes, as she gave no resistance to letting him merge his thoughts with her own. He lay down next to her as they fell into deep sleep, where he could Dream them both into the past.

NINE

There were too many memories of Cirrus that Nafury had to choose from. It was hard for him to pick one on the spot as something that would make Ubi see Cirrus the same way he had. He thought back into his past, to a time before he was controlled by Daath. He looked up and ahead to find himself leaning against the Fay Wall. He didn't know what he was thinking about back then, other than the only thing he wanted. A miracle. An answer. Something. But nothing had come to him in his Visions. The Novaists whose beautiful voices echoed from inside the Fay Wall gave little comfort. Nafury didn't see in the past that Cirrus was standing at the end of the Halls of Aragmoth watching him. He only saw him now. His friend was a piece of the miracle that he needed. Ubi stood near him, examining the memory with interest. She saw Cirrus moments after he did.

"That's him?" Ubi asked.

"Yes," Nafury replied.

"He's beautiful," Ubi thought aloud. Everything in this Dream of the past would be heard from her thoughts either way.

Cirrus had helped Nafury obtain his shift at the bottom of the Eternal Waters. It was a horribly deformed and a wretched form of a brownish-black dragon. It hurt Nafury to see his best friend shift out of his beautiful, human-like appearance and into his white dragon form. He tried to will Cirrus to not shift without saying it to him as their eyes met. It seemed to work. Cirrus' Curse of being trapped since birth in the form of a dragon was broken. It saddened Nafury that he only knew now that it had never been a Curse, but Alexia containing him. Years later to date of this memory, Cirrus was still catching up on all the cues and human habits that came with being a dragoon. But it was the untamed form of him that was his truth, and the one Nafury preferred to look at. The dragon and not the human-like dragoon he was trying so hard to be.

Today Cirrus seemed to try even harder, as he straightened up and withdrew his staring at the Prince. Maybe he had seen something that Nafury couldn't. This was just a memory, as it was impossible to change it to make it possible for Cirrus to see Ubi as he could. All he could do is re-enact it all in hopes of seeing something that he missed before. He feared the hidden hate that Ubi likely held for Cirrus, and he wanted it resolved now. While there was still time. She blamed Cirrus for taking her mother from Kas' side, and he had to change that. Cirrus was dead now, but how he was remembered also mattered the world to Nafury. "Can you see it?"

"See what?" Cirrus asked as he walked closer.

"Our kind has struggled for centuries to gain the blessing of Aragmoth, yet he has done nothing but ignore our prayers. Even his wing tries to fold its touch away from us."

"You're tired and need to rest," Cirrus replied.

"If we brought the Asterian Caelestis here, he would not be able to ignore us any longer. This can be the only reason why I was made to look like this. It's all a test."

"You are still beautiful, Nafury. Stop talking like you're different."

"I am not beautiful, and you can hide your soul within your shift all you want. You insult me by thinking I can't see your intent to try and make me feel better."

"That's not true," Cirrus replied.

"We are all beautiful in the eyes of those who love us, and I can feel your love for me more than anyone else's. But if I had her love, then there would be no need for anyone to pity me. I would have everything I could ever need. Only fools look down on those blessed by Aragmoth, and she can set me free. Help me bring her here, Cirrus."

"The only way to her is the Gate in Mer City and she would die from the pressure."

"Not if inside one of our shifts. But she would never see past this deformed monstrosity I have been made into to give my love for her a chance. I can't do it alone," Nafury pleaded.

"Nafury, just stop! It's too dangerous, and I can't—I won't do this."

"Then you are no different from the rest of them!" Nafury snapped angrily back at him. He brought his teeth together in a clash of unevenness and pain. It angered him that this memory was not the perfect one he needed now. "You claim to love and care for me, yet you hide under the shadow of doubt my father casts over everyone! You are nothing but a lie!" It was then that Nafury lost control of his body in his rage and charged straight at him. He struck Cirrus with his dragon claws hard enough to shatter his body against a pillar.

Nafury had completely forgotten for that critical moment that he was in his dragon form in this memory. When Cirrus fell to the ground, Nafury fell with him and out of his shift, praying that he hadn't killed him. Nafury remembered not understanding how he had been able to hit him at all. The Laws of Aragmoth didn't allow shifts to attack souls. Not unless they were an immediate threat.

Nafury lifted Cirrus' head from the pillar. Several

pieces of white stone fell to the ground near them. Blood stained Cirrus' long, blond hair and now Nafury's hand. Cirrus started to come around and immediately pulled Nafury against his chest. He was alive, and just as broken and confused. "Cirrus, I'm sorry—!"

"This is just a mistake. I must have been too angry or something."

Nafury knew that he should have been the one paralyzed in pain. That was the minor punishment for doing something like this. But he couldn't feel Aragmoth's wrath. He knew then that he was not like Cirrus. He was something else entirely. He just didn't know then that he was a half human, half demon capable of turning Aster into a frozen wasteland.

"Are you alright?" Cirrus asked.

Nafury shuddered at the question. Cirrus was worried about him when he had nearly killed him. "Just a mistake." Nafury shuddered again, before the realization that the back of his shirt was wet. The wounds that Nafury's father had whipped into his back had reopened and now bled.

Cirrus used his aeri to heal them as he had dozens of times before. It was as if Cirrus blamed himself for every wound on Nafury, many of which opened without warning. Dreamwalking was dangerous and deadly. The Sentry of Earth took no prisoners from the souls from Aster who dared to walk across their world. But it was the only way Nafury could see the Caelestis, and he didn't care what it cost. Except every time that Cirrus touched him. Nafury had paid for his Dreamwalking by means of Simera's punishment more times than he could remember. The scars on his back never completely healed. Nafury pulled away from Cirrus and got to his feet. "I'll be at the wind tunnels."

"I'll escort you back," Cirrus said and got up.

He needs to be remembered, Nafury thought as he waited until Cirrus was gone. He looked then to where Ubi continued to watch in silence. "That's not a memory I wanted you to see." He lowered his head then in shame. He couldn't tell what she was thinking with his own thoughts everywhere.

"No memory is perfect," she replied, and looked away from Nafury and to the floor. She walked over to him and set a hand on his back. The wounds from the whip Simera had inflicted on him still hurt. "I suppose I should be grateful he never hit me."

Nafury looked away from her and to where Cirrus had left down the hall. "He thought of Cirrus as a second son, when all along he was the real one. I can't help but wonder if Simera knew."

Ubi looked to where Nafury did and pondered on it with him. "He never mentioned him. Yet he never mentioned anyone on Aster. It didn't take a genius to tell that Simera was an alien. Despite that, he was content to keep the existence of Aster a secret from me entirely."

Nafury felt a dark shadow drift past the Threads between them and looked back at her. She was a good liar, but she wasn't perfect. "How far does your hate stretch on this world?"

Ubi looked up at him as his unexpected change in tone frightened her. "What do you mean?"

"You were cast out of the first Aster. Theoretically, you should hate this one just as much."

Ubi lowered her gaze to the stone floor. "I hate a lot of things. I regret even more. What Xirel said is right but he's also wrong about one important thing."

Nafury waited for her to continue.

"I already remember everything. I remember every time the Sentry killed me all the way back to my father bringing me to Earth and leaving me there."

"Do you deceive Xirel and me then?"

Ubi shook her head. "It's all so exhausting. Holding onto all that hate and fear all the time. But with you and Xirel, I'm less scared. I don't know if I can ever belong on this world, but I want to stay with you. If only to see what life can be like when you're not going through it alone. I can't guarantee that I will always be like this. I might even become some vengeful destroyer of a monster one day, but it won't be today."

Nafury kissed her forehead, then brushed some of her dark bangs from her eyes. "I definitely have to recommend avoiding the monster route. Destroying the world can leave you rather lonely."

Ubi shook her head as he tried to cheer her up by making fun of it. "I can feel your love for Cirrus, even though none of it belongs to me," she said and pressed her fists to her chest. She rested her head against him, trying to decipher the code from his heartbeat. "Do you think Cirrus would have liked me?"

"Heh," Nafury said and rested his chin on her head. "I think you both would have gotten along well. Both of you are completely unruly."

Ubi smiled and then looked around as their surroundings suddenly faded and changed. They were on a field of flowers now. Only the petals were soaked in blood. The field was covered with the bodies of plumas and dragoons who had taken back to their human form. Dozens on dozens of spirits stayed by their souls, unable to do anything more for them.

Nafury hadn't conjured this memory. He looked at Ubi who didn't have any idea how it appeared, either. "Alexia must be messing with us."

"What is this memory?" Ubi asked in concern of the death that surrounded them. It was a complete nightmare of a sight.

They both looked to where a silver-armored man stood on the edge of the canyon. From his long, blond hair, Nafury thought it might be Cirrus. He walked over to him and the man turned to face him.

"You will keep her from me no longer!" the man threatened. Then the knight unsheathed his blade and lashed out at Nafury with it.

TEN

Nafury woke with a start and immediately looked for Ubi. He found her, still locked in a restless sleep. He gently shook her until she opened her eyes and was free of the nightmare.

"What was that all about?" Ubi asked as she sat up and rubbed her eyes.

"I don't know. I do know that Cirrus never raised a weapon to me, ever."

"Scary," Ubi said as she tried to figure out the nightmare's hidden message.

"Fay are supposed to be able to see into the future as well as the past. Maybe we drew his angry spirit too close to us instead of your mother's."

"Maybe," Ubi theorized. "He did mention a 'her.' Whatever the meaning of it is, I want to go see if Xirel is alright. I had enough sleep for now."

Nafury followed after her. After some minutes, they tracked down Xirel to a small conference-like room. If he hadn't the ability to sense the Awl's Threads, they might have roamed the massive mountain forever. The chimera Awl was speaking with another when they entered. He couldn't help but stare at the newcomer's light green hair. *It can't be...*

"Hello," the Awl said politely and turned to face them. "Prince Nafury. And this must be our newest Fay. It's an honour," he continued and looked to Ubi, before finishing his greeting with a short bow.

Nafury hadn't been called a Prince for so long, he almost didn't recognize his former title. He was frozen in shock to see Loki. The last time he had seen the Awl dragoon was on Earth, right after Sybl's fall. The only thing that kept Loki from strangling him with his bare hands back then was likely Hino and the once-Sentry's inability to hurt a human. Whatever Loki was thinking at that moment remained hidden under his silver mask that covered his eyes.

"I am Loki," the orange-eyed Awl added. "At your service."

"Loki is the leader of the Eastern Tribes," Xirel elaborated. "I contacted him with our desire to head over to the Torian Continent. He has a ship that can take us over. It has the added security of several Awls should the dragons prove to be less hospitable than usual."

"Where have you been all this time?" Nafury asked and took a step forward.

Loki looked to the side for a moment before looking back at him. "I swore that I would never forgive you after what happened to Sybl. That was until I finally came to realize that I was just as much at fault as you."

"How so?" Nafury asked.

"I swore to her that I would protect her, and I wasn't there when she needed me the most. But when I look at her," Loki said, nodding towards Ubi, "I see a second chance."

"I must thank you then. Especially as my plan is still a work in progress."

Loki returned a fleeting smile. "If a war can be adverted, then it is worth a try. We cannot leave any negotiations to the Atrum. The dragons will not care what burns should they make the trip over to this Continent. You and I both know this. I can sense Sybl's spirit close to us, so this journey will fair well."

"You can sense her?" Nafury asked, intrigued. "Even though she's in the realm of death?"

Loki's smile grew and he looked at Xirel as they quietly guarded the secret between them.

"Is there a reason we can't be brought in on the secret?" Ubi asked, not enjoying being left out of the loop.

"First you must master Thread before you can understand, Princess. Please understand that we only hold from you what you are not yet able to comprehend," Loki said.

Ubi crossed her arms before her, not pleased with his answer.

"Okay then..." Nafury said and gently ushered Ubi out of the room before she could lose her cool on Loki. He called in question back as they left, "When do we leave?"

"Whenever you are ready," Xirel replied and got up from the chair he sat in.

Nafury pulled Ubi towards the exit. He quickly distracted her with how she would love the Harbor's shopping. Outside, he was surprised to find Sial waiting for them. "Oh joy, my spirit guide is back. That can only mean that I'm due to get a life-threatening situation soon."

"It's a unicorn," Ubi said as she looked Sial over again. The kyrie didn't so much as flinch as she touched him. "She's rather smart for an animal."

"He comes like that," Nafury replied.

Ubi looked into Sial's purple eyes. She quickly lost the staring contest. "That's creepy when I think about it. An animal that is as intelligent as a human, Eminor or Ancient?"

"He is very old. His Thread tornado isn't something anyone can learn in a single lifetime," Nafury said and walked over to Sial. He stopped when Ubi brought her hand to her chin in thought. "What is it?"

"Well, it's just that you keep saying 'him' and Sial is

clearly a girl."

Nafury laughed at her like she were mad. "Sial has never been or ever will be a girl."

"Seriously? You had this kyrie close to you how long and you can't tell its gender?"

Nafury's intelligence took a direct hit, so he took a few steps back to confirm that Sial was a male. Only, the kyrie was indeed lacking certain parts. Now he was creeped out. "Um, Sial, are you feeling okay?"

"You are unbelievable," Ubi said.

Nafury hesitated to follow, as he felt Loki come out to join them. "Loki, is Sial a male or female?"

Loki lifted an eyebrow, clearly amused. "Are you unable to tell?"

"He was a male. He has always been a male —" Nafury stopped when he looked back at Loki. Their escort to the Harbor had shifted into his light green dragon form. He hadn't grown at all, and was easily still half of Nafury's dragon size. Loki sat down and waited patiently for the rest of his words. "All that command over Thread and you're still puny?"

'Of all the things to be exorcised from you, the jerk part of you had to stick, didn't it?' "Princess," Loki said by voice then and looked at the Fay, "did he get any sleep? He seems rather grouchy."

"You might be right. We should leave him behind," Ubi teased.

Nafury continued to wait where he was for Xirel to emerge from the mountain. "Xirel, what is going on?"

Xirel shifted into his stag form and shook out his white coat. "It is as they said, you clearly need more sleep." He kneeled down so Ubi could pull herself up behind him, and started for the Harbor with Loki right behind, following by air.

Nafury was officially agitated. "That coming from the one who says I sleep too much... Would it kill you to make up your mind!?"

'Sial is a male. Or at least, he was a male,' Alexia spoke to his psi.

"So I'm not crazy," Nafury replied, but remained determined to get the answers he wanted. Sial had never been a female—he knew that because he had fashioned the beast himself millennium ago. When it was reincarnated through Nephena, the Ancient was still a male.

He caught the creature's horn in his hand and forced its purple eyes to look into his. Closing his eyes, he then traced the Threads of its horn back into its memories. This demanded answers.

Nafury opened his eyes to find himself in the past. The Atrum that towered before him was like a spire-shaped tomb that reached into the sky. Nothing of it in this age made it look like the center of the Suzerain Continent that it had become. Before and during the Last War, Atrum City was little more than a shanty town. One filled with criminals, Feharin, and shifters who didn't fit in anywhere. He walked towards the Atrum for a while, until he spotted the one he looked for. *Sybl.*

She sensed him before she heard his thoughts and turned around. "Who is Sybl?"

Nafury cleared his throat and looked himself over. This was a memory of the past, and the sister he knew in the present was not here in consciousness form. This was Asil, Sybl's previous incarnation. "What are you doing here alone?"

"I wanted to see you," she started.

"I'm here," he said and walked closer. The memory of Asil before him didn't know him yet as the monster Daath that he had become. Nothing of her showed any fear of him.

"You're not wearing your armor," she said, trying to lighten the air between them.

Nafury took notice of that on her mentioning. He didn't look much like the Damek he was playing the part of in this reenactment. "After what happened between us, I didn't feel like fighting anymore." He looked then at the shadows that hid nearby, daring them to just try and take him on today.

"I had no right to get angry at you like that. The phelan are beautiful and powerful creatures for battle.

They are even more magnificent than the Nightmare Eaters of the first Aster," Asil said.

"They are yours," he said, pulling his festra from his back and handing it to her.

"They're your army," Asil said, but took the weapon anyway.

Nafury shook his head. "All this has shown me that the choices I would have made on the first Aster are not suitable choices for this one. This is your world. I gave this to Asteria once, so the names bound to this weapon are now your army. You can make new wishes, but you cannot alter the ones made in your past. My most significant wish will always be for the happiness of my most beautiful Fay. You will always belong to me." Asil stood her ground as he touched the side of her face and kissed her forehead. Unlike this memory with Sybl, it didn't send a freezing chill down her spine. A feeling of warmth and safety blushed Asil's cheeks instead. "I wish I could go back and do everything right the first time. I wish you could only know me as I am now and never as anything else."

She tilted her head as she studied his expression. "You seem so distant today. What's bothering you? You know you can tell me."

"I know, and I know you would do everything in your power to make it right. But this is something that I need to do alone," he said. "In the meantime, I need you to promise me something."

"Of course," Asil replied.

"I need you to promise that you will always remember me. Just as I am now, regardless of what I become in the future."

"You are the last one I would ever forget about, Damek. Now stop being so serious—you're making me worry."

"I'm sorry," he said and turned around. When he walked away, the memory faded behind him. He opened his eyes and found himself standing before Sial, still holding onto his horn. He wasn't sure how long he had been away for, as snow had begun to pile up at his feet. Alexia had let him get rather cold, as her patience for him had expired.

"You want what can never be, Damek," she stated without reserve.

"I want Sybl to be happy and safe, as I have always wanted. I have no more demons left for excuses to keep me from achieving just that." He pulled Alexia's spirit to him, and shifted into his dragon form. Spreading his white wings out with a small cry, he used his aeri in the Threads of wind around him to warm up his blood. Retaking his command over the air, he turned his wings for the Harbor.

ELEVEN

Xirel watched Ubi run from one vendor to the next in the market at the Harbor. She was taking in everything that other-world shopping had to offer and not wearing out any time soon. He checked that he still carried all his money with him, just to be safe. The GLORIA would be the ship to take them over to the Torian Continent, and its captain had yet to negotiate all the costs of such trip.

According to Loki, no ship had made the trip in years. Cecil had taken leadership of the dragons by right of his bloodline of Moon. While he did talk with friends of Sybl and the Sanctus, it didn't last long after her death. He only kept talks out of respect for Master Gei of the Sanctus. The Iynx had brought Cecil's Rose back to him from the ashes of the Phoenix's downfall. Just as the Sanctus decayed, so did Cecil's patience for the Suzerain Continent. The warmongering that had taken up much of

Kenshe's time made the phelan a nuisance. It was a campaign of fear, not security that he offered. It was likely the best he could do with his predecessor being the perfect dark Fay, Kas.

Xirel's reminiscing of the past had distracted him. He brought his attention back to the present and found that Ubi wasn't where he last saw her. He could once again hear the fighting for first buying rights around him. The healing plants brought back from the Torian Continent would sell for a fortune. He lifted his hand to find Ubi's Threads, before turning around on feeling she was right behind him. In her hands, she held up a thin, dark blue cloak that was well sewn.

"You need to buy this for me."

"Ubi..." Xirel let out a sigh. It wasn't that he didn't want to buy it, it was that it was his least favourite colour.

"I can't wear my black one on the Torian Continent, cause the merchant said it will be too warm. Please please."

"Did you have to find one the same sapphire colour as your uncle's eyes?"

Ubi lowered her hands and looked closer at the cloak on Xirel's mentioning of Nafury. Then she let out an even more enthusiastic, "Yes!"

"Master Xirel?" a voice said from beside him.

"Yes?" Xirel replied and turned around to look at the young man.

"The captain is ready to go when you are."

"We will be right there," Xirel said and looked back at Ubi, as her eyes had grown larger with her plea to have the cloak. It didn't help that she made them glow blue, targeting his weakness. He reluctantly gave in and handed her a few coins to give to the merchant. She dashed off to pay for it, then put it on right after and came running back to him. "If the meals on the ship prove to not be free, you are going to be learning to use Thread to fish for your dinner."

Ubi laughed and followed him as they walked for the ship and across its plank. The captain was a stocky short man who had purchased the GLORIA after its former captain's death. Ubi wasn't sure if he was a human or some kind of shifter, as there was just too much going on to pinpoint all the shifts. The captain called for castoff, and immediately the ship turned into a machine of well-abled men. They started swiftly on their designated tasks without hesitation. Because of the escort to be had, the best of the best were on board to serve on this venture.

Most of the Awls who had not been killed during the Aeger had retreated into hiding or joined the Atrum's Order. Those who had sided with Kenshe were later chased out and took refuge in the established Awl Tribes. Loki's Tribe was such a place for some years now. No one had a death wish to go near the Continent of dragons. Xirel and Loki were a rare blessing of protection to the ship. This soon became evident when the crew attended to him and Ubi as if they were royalty. Xirel smiled as he watched Ubi raise her head high in her new cloak. It made him happy to see her free her mind and worries from her inner demons long enough to have some fun. He wondered how long he could hold onto the Ubi before him now.

Xirel went over to the rail and looked back at the Suzerain Continent that disappeared from sight. The fog of the estus energy that surrounded the land was as a thick, dark blanket created by the Aur. It would set soon, and the Soph Aur of Toria would rise with its bright light and cover the atmosphere with colour. A sharp stab of pain struck Xirel's heart, and he immediately looked around for the attacker. Only no one had struck him but his own sad reminiscing. There were no more Aur storms to endanger their journey. The Sylvan Aur brought balance to the Soph and Atrum's Aur. It was also why his Caelestis had to remain in the realm of death.

Sial had not brought Nafury to the Harbor yet when they had set sail. His brother had sent word by psi that he would make his way on his own to them. Xirel silently prayed that he didn't make a huge mistake by leaving Nafury alone with Alexia. He didn't want Nafury to be the first dragon he had to tear from the skies on their journey. Xirel once believed that Sybl's brother should have been executed for his crimes. Now he found that he had changed his mind. He was Ubi's only real family left here on Aster. For that reason, he convinced himself to continue to try and befriend Nafury. It wasn't like the human was completely useless anymore, at least.

'You're too hard on yourself, Xirel. It will be okay.'

He smiled as a memory of Sybl's words touched his mind and eased the pain he felt. She wasn't completely gone, and he only had to keep reminding himself of that. Fay didn't die. She would stay with Aragmoth until he was healed and Aster was once again in balance. He hoped that he would still be alive the day she chose to return, if she did at all.

"Incoming dragon! All hands on deck—wait—is that the White Death...?" the captain trailed off.

All the Threads on the ship all vibrated fear at once as the white titan flew straight towards them. Xirel found Ubi and pulled her close as he lifted his hand in the ready. He would cut the Threads of the dragon's wings should Nafury have lost his soul to Alexia. But the dragon did not attack and slowed his approach.

Nafury manipulated the air around himself until him could hover close enough to unshift and land his feet on deck. Such a feat would have been impossible for a dragon with no power over wind. Xirel lowered his hand and let out a breath of relief, as the entire ship remained in absolute panic.

"Nafury!" Ubi squealed and ran over to him. "You made it!"

"Of course I did. So little faith," he said as he looked at Xirel who raised an eyebrow at him, clearly unimpressed.

"Was it necessary to terrify the entire ship?" Xirel asked.

"Sorry, I was never much of a swimmer," Nafury replied with a shrug. He avoided eye contact with the crew that was now really angry. A few had soiled themselves from the fear of dying moments ago.

"Master Xirel, is he a...friend?" the captain asked, hobbling over to them.

"Indeed. Tell your men that they have nothing to fear now, as a dragoon and two Awls will be escorting them."

"Phew. I didn't know there was another white dragon on Aster," the captain replied. The stocky man wiped the sweat from his forehead with his dirty handkerchief.

"There has only ever been one white dragon on Aster," Xirel replied.

The captain's eyes darted back at Nafury, before he made a hasty retreat to his cabin. He seemed uninterested in further details.

"And to think you scold me for terrifying them," Nafury said.

"You can't blame their terror," Loki said as he jumped down from an overhead mast. "You left little to the imagination of Simera back at the Sanctus."

Nafury had yet to question Alexia of what had all transpired at the Sanctus. She was overly quiet about the topic.

'I may have overdone it a little...' Alexia psi admitted.

"Your crazed shift even cowers at the reality of what she did," Loki said. "They are still looking for all the body parts. I don't know what Alexia's history is with Simera, yet I think we should hear it before we continue on."

Alexia? Nafury asked, and found her near the cabin wall. She couldn't become entirely invisible to him.

She didn't answer.

Nafury became more determined with his psi barrage on her, but she gave up nothing. Loki joined Nafury's efforts with his own psi and raised the pressure, and after a few minutes she buckled and gave in. Her usually cool, collected thoughts were now disorientated, as if she had hit her head. They saw enough, and Nafury let her be as she retreated from the deck.

Nafury closed his eyes for a moment to let the sickening truth sink in. Even Loki had a look of shock on his face now. "He had what was coming for him," Nafury said and focused on Ubi who was listening to everything next to him.

Xirel got the message that what happened to Alexia was not something for a young woman's ears when Loki looked at him. He left with the Awl to do other things.

Nafury focused on Ubi and brought a hasty change of

subject. "I like your cloak." He straightened the hood on her head, and brushed some of her bangs out of her eyes.

"Xirel almost didn't buy it for me." Ubi pretended to pout. "He said that he would only show me how to use Thread to fish!"

Nafury laughed and shook his head. "By the caels, you found his sense of humour. There are still miracles to be found on Aster."

"You will teach me how to read the Thread so I can see the memories of my necklace, right?" Ubi asked.

"Maybe. But fishing can be fun too," Nafury teased as he leaned over the rail to get a closer view of the blue water.

Ubi kicked him in the backside almost hard enough to push him over.

"Okay okay," Nafury surrendered and sat down on the rail instead. "What did you want to learn first? Lifelines? Reading minds? Manipulating objects? Killing small animals?"

Ubi replied with a mean glare.

"Okay, we can leave out killing anything," he teased.

Ubi thought on the choices for a moment. "Reading minds. I think that trick would be handy."

"Alright, I will be your test mouse for this assignment. People and shifters usually have at least one thought in common. In a fight, it's defence and offence. In a conversation, it's often the theme of what is being talked about. Ultimately, every one has a thought that can be seen and read from their psi. When you learn the basics, you can expand beyond that and see even more of their thoughts."

"Unless they block you out, right?" Ubi asked.

"Yes. If they don't trust you, then that creates a lot of walls to jump and it makes it more tiring. Losing your mental strength jumping these barriers can leave your mind vulnerable in turn."

"I think that makes sense. So what do I do?" Ubi asked.

"Well, we have a few things in common. Try and see what I'm thinking. I won't put up any barriers, which is pointless as our Awls have already read me inside and out." Nafury sighed.

Ubi giggled and then became focused on his eyes, searching for the one thought that would link her mind to his. She was having a hard time, and it was likely because Xirel was watching her from nearby. "Why is he staring at me?"

"He must be bored. Hey, I have an idea," Nafury said as a devious smile crept up on his face. "All chimeras have a deformity of some sort. Xirel's is proving particularly difficult for me to find."

"You think that I could read his mind and find it?" Ubi asked, now wearing a devious look to match his.

"I can't get anywhere near his head. He deals

headaches out rather ruthlessly. But he won't hurt you."

Ubi accepted the challenge as she went over to Xirel. The Awl was already well aware of their evil plan to uncover his secret deformity.

"Xirel," Ubi said, as if she was about to scold him for something.

"Ubi," Xirel replied. "Uncovering the thoughts of an Awl is not as easy as your uncle would have you believe."

"Well, then it won't hurt for me to practice."

Xirel nodded and smiled as he could feel her thoughts focus entirely on him with her blue eyes. Without training, her psi was random at best as it tried to seek out what she wanted from his mind. It was effortless for him to navigate her thoughts away from her intended target. He stood patiently and waited for her to admit defeat, and decided to watch her fairy pendant on her neck for a while. He could feel the long Threads of memories within its gold and wondered if she would let him look at it later. It twisted in place, and his mind came back to the present.

"Aha! Nafury! I found it!" Ubi exclaimed. She then caught Xirel's white shirt before he could refocus on her and lifted it. Xirel's pale face went completely red as her fingers carefully counted his ribs. "This is it—you don't have all your ribs! I found his weakness! He's missing ribs!"

Some of the crew had stopped what they were doing from her loud excitement. After a few moments they realized that it was a false alarm, and a few laughed it off before returning to their work.

Xirel lowered his shirt and straightened it out. Then he regained his posture that Ubi's touch had melted down. He looked at Nafury who still sat on the rail, looking completely unsatisfied with the answer Ubi had uncovered.

"That's it? Just a few ribs? What the heck, Xirel?" Nafury said.

"Would you rather I was missing some other body part?"

"Yeah," Nafury grunted in an unserious tone and jumped down to the deck. "Like...everything."

"I did it!" Ubi squealed as she ran back to Nafury.

"Not bad at all for a first try," he said and patted her head once. "Tomorrow we work on basic lifelines. Or lack thereof." He didn't need to look at Xirel to make it clear he was referring to him.

"Alright. I'm gonna catch a nap," Ubi said and headed off.

"A nap? Just how much shopping did you guys do?" Nafury asked in concern as he watched her go below deck. He had never seen her go to sleep without a fight till now.

Xirel was rubbing his shirt now, as if to remove something invisible.

"You going to be alright?" Nafury asked. "We're

surrounded by cold water if you need some."

Xirel realized what he was doing and stopped. Ignoring Nafury's comment he said, "I hope you don't have any extended plans for our visit to the Torian Continent...?"

"I promised our lady Fay a castle. I intend to keep my promise."

"So certain of your strength already?" Xirel asked. "It is still several hundred dragons against one berserker."

"I never said that I wouldn't appreciate some help, particularly as she just wants to see it." Nafury ran his hand through his hair then to brush back some of the worries that had yet to catch up to his thoughts.

TWELVE

Nafury found Ubi already fast asleep on a hammock below deck. He decided to sit down next to her. He used to be able to see into the future through his own Dreams, but it was something he had lost since losing Daath. A part of him wondered if the demon had taken that ability of his into oblivion. Now he pondered trespassing into Ubi's mind. He was curious to what she saw. Fay were supposed to be able to see both the past and future. As a dark Fay, she likely could see the future best. He made up his mind and closed his eyes, then used his psi to find where Ubi's thoughts might have wandered off to.

He wandered through several foggy scenes for a while. Eventually, he found Ubi sitting before a screen of images.

We have confirmed, the attack on Central is centered around what appears to be a dragon. Authorities are working with the army on just how to take down the creature that is causing unprecedented chaos downtown.

Nafury watched the image of himself on the screen as he was when he was possessed by Daath. He was terrifying.

This just in! Our cameras have spotted a young woman on the rooftop with the monster! She appears to be holding on just barely! Oh no —she has lost her grip!

Screams consumed the air then as the camera followed Sybl's fall. But his sister vanished in a blink of stars before she could collide with the ground. Nafury's eyes were already closed. This wasn't the future, but a past he had hoped to never see again.

Ubi turned around and looked at him. He struggled to regain himself as he didn't realize that he had started to cry. She got up and went over to him and hugged him, catching him completely off guard. "I know you didn't kill my mother and that you were possessed by Daath at the time. I forgive you if you tell me that this is true."

Nafury touched her long, dark hair as she pressed her face into his chest. He feared her hot tears would burn his heart right out of him. "I make no excuses for my weakness and inability to keep it from happening. I should be the one who is dead, not your mother. Nothing I do can ever redeem me for what I've done." Ubi pulled away from him and he wiped some of the tears out of her eyes with his cold thumb. "So I don't want you to forgive me, ever. What I do know is that if your mother had known of your existence, she would have turned Earth inside out to find you."

"I know that now," Ubi said. "It's what you almost did. Had she remembered me, she would have likely helped you in its destruction. I can and I will forgive you, but I will never forget what Earth and its Sentry have done to all of us. I don't ever want to go back, but I don't want to put you and Xirel in danger by being here."

"Heh," Nafury replied. "Trouble is like my own personal shadow, anyways. Maybe the three of us stand a better chance at keeping it at bay."

Ubi smiled and touched the pendant on her neck. "I have a family now," she said optimistically. "We are family. I won't let them take you or Xirel from me."

"Same," Nafury assured her. "We all have a hundred secrets, a hundred regrets, and a thousand demons. But if we are honest with each other, I know we will be alright. Even if the truth is as painful as this. Can you promise me that?"

Ubi nodded and looked back at the screen as the memory of the news broadcast faded and left grey static on the screen. "I was so young at the time, but I remember this sickening feeling in my stomach when I saw this. Only when she was gone did the memory return to me that she was my mother. I rushed downtown to try and find something—anything of her, but I found nothing. It was complete chaos, even after the Asterians left. That was when the Sentry found me and put me in an asylum. I guess because of what my mother did made them not want to kill me right there. Or maybe it was because of the dragons being there, I don't know."

"If only Sybl would have told me you existed before she died. It wasn't until she spoke to me as a spirit shortly after that I learned of you," Nafury said and looked to the ground. "I might have been able to save you sooner."

"It's okay, cause it all worked out now. Besides, I probably would have killed you if you came near me back then."

"I suppose you're right," Nafury said.

"Fay govern the will of Aragmoth, and therefore Aster. Of course I'm right."

"Has Xirel inflated your head that much already?" Nafury laughed.

"Hey!" she snapped back. "You watch, when I learn how to use Thread, Aragmoth will listen to me too."

"I don't doubt it in the slightest, Mistress over Awls," Nafury mocked. She punched his arm rather hard. It was enough to wake them from sleep in a fit of laughter.

"What in blazes is going on down here?" Xirel asked from the stairs.

Nafury and Ubi only laughed harder, till she finally curled up and returned to sleep.

Xirel just shook his head as he looked at Nafury.

"Caelestis save us all. Their madness has reached the point of laughing at their nightmares..."

"Lighten up you old grump," Nafury said and got to his feet. "It's going to be alright." Xirel's purple eyes suddenly grew wide and Nafury froze for moment. Then he looked around for what might have stumped the Awl so bad. He didn't think till now that it was even possible to surprise an Awl. "What is it?"

The normal Xirel came back around and shook his head. "It is nothing. I am going back on deck."

"By the way, did we have a plan for if we get outnumbered over there?"

"Yes, you just reminded me of it actually," Xirel replied.

"Oh?"

"We pray."

THIRTEEN

It took Kenshe over a week to recover from the Fay's attack. His own shift had inflicted a near-lethal amount of damage to him. He was still on edge as none of his training as a Custos prepared him for any of it. He had been born like a True—he never thought that one day he would be almost eaten by one. He closed his eyes and found his thoughts drifting to those of Nafury. Something had struck the Threads between them hard enough to get his attention.

"Lord Kenshe," Feryl's voice said from across the table. The council members in the room had taken notice of the Atrum Lord's lack of attention.

Kenshe blinked and pulled his focus from whatever the hell Nafury was doing now to the present.

"You heard it too, didn't you? Just now?" Prisca asked from where she stood looking out the window of the War

Room.

Kenshe looked at his most devoted ayame, who was always one step ahead of him. She rarely missed the chance to be by his side since she was just a little girl watching him from her windowsill. He had almost lost her to death by Simera at the Sanctus. Had he been a minute more late, she would have died from the amount of blood she lost. That had scared him. The sight of the berserking White Death at the Sanctus had terrified him even more. With some luck, the monster would stay on the Torian Continent. And there was still a Fay out there capable of killing him. He had more fears than he could conjure solutions for as of late. He never felt the need for Sybl's or Kas' guidance as much as he did now. Kenshe shoved his never-ending worries out of the way and brought his thoughts back to the discussion at hand. "How many Callers can we get back to the Atrum before morning?"

"We will have at least fifty by then," Prisca replied.

"That won't be enough to cover the Harbor and the City from the dragons," Kenshe calculated out loud. We will have to evacuate the Harbor. Send out the Call."

"Of all the things," Feryl grumbled, "why does it have to be dragons? The Awls are enough to deal with." He didn't waste time waiting for answers that weren't available and left the War Room.

Prisca's chilling Call went out across the Threads, reaching every ayame for miles. She too shared Kenshe's belief that this day was inevitable. Sybl's sacrifice had only given them a temporary peace.

"I will have to get my hands on Nafury for the entire story of what's going on," Kenshe said.

"That's dangerous," Prisca said as she followed Kenshe out of the War Room. "If he goes berserk on you, he could kill you."

"I know, but I have an idea. But it's going to take the whole Pack to make it work."

They continued downstairs to the main hall. Feryl, Tank, and the others of his Pack were there waiting.

"Boss, what are we doing?" Feryl asked in concern.

Kenshe looked towards the entrance where Tank leaned against the frame. "Nafury isn't going to help us out, so I'm going to have to bite it out of their Fay. If he does decide to bring the dragons back here, I will kill him first."

"She almost killed you once now," Tank replied. "Then there's no telling what her blood will do to you. Sybl's blood could heal, but I'm willing to bet that a dark Fay's will poison."

"That's a chance I have to take. She won't know it's me this time until I have what I want from her. You will all have to distract Nafury in the meantime," Kenshe instructed.

"Alright," Feryl replied and started out of the Atrum, followed by the others. "I think I'll go grab Nafury's helmet real quick."

FOURTEEN

Nafury fell into a deep sleep to the sound of gentle waves from an uneventful week. It was a long journey across the Eternal Waters to the Torian Continent. What he didn't expect was for Ubi to drop in on his own Dreams like he had hers. In what he hoped would be a Dream this time around, he found himself on the same field where Cirrus had attacked him. Nafury turned from watching the woman across the field to where Ubi took up his side.

"That's my mother, isn't it?" Ubi asked.

"Yes, but this isn't from my memories. I think it's one of Alexia's. We should go."

"Please, let me see her first."

"Ubi..." Nafury wasn't in the mood to take any chances again. If that was Asil before them, then it could spell disaster for Ubi to see her mother when she was hailed as a goddess of war. Not remembering her own daughter could prove to be the least of their worries if Asil tried to kill them here. Such a nightmare would be impossible to forget.

"I know she won't recognize me. But it's okay if only I remember her," Ubi said.

It all felt like a bad idea, but Nafury reluctantly agreed and went over with Ubi.

Sybl turned around as they approached and smiled at Nafury, then looked at Ubi beside him. "It's hard to believe that you are already the age I was when I first came to Aster. It is good to see you, daughter."

"Mom!" Ubi exclaimed and hesitated for a moment before closing the gap between them with a hug.

"Sybl?" Nafury asked, feeling that this wasn't a Dream of the past at all anymore.

"You're the one who wondered what would happen if two Dreamwalkers dreamt the same thing. Reality doesn't seem so wonderful in comparison to how real of a place mere thoughts can create." Sybl looked across the chasm of the Casus Beli field. It looked to stretch as far as she was able to remember it could.

Nafury had come to believe that dreams should always be just out of reach. For if you catch them and they shatter in your hands, then you will have lost everything. For there will be nothing left to pull yourself out of the nightmares with. Now, his one chance to stop it all from happening again stood right before him. She hadn't aged a day, where he was now twenty-six. "It's good to see you."

"You are turning into an old man," Sybl mocked, looking him over. "And you," Sybl said and looked at Ubi, "look so much like Kas I could cry." She smiled and closed her eyes for a moment. "I know it's hard, but I want you to forgive him for what he did."

Ubi's face changed instantly to a hateful expression on the suggestion. "I can't do that. He banished me to one short lifetime after the other filled with suffering and death!"

"I know that now," Sybl said, and brushed some of Ubi's dark hair back from her shoulder.

"He took me from you! Now you're dead and...and..!"

"Hey," Sybl said and pulled Ubi to her and into a hug. "You have to let the hate go, or our enemies will use it against you. Kas was a Fay of darkness, just like you. But unlike you he didn't have the emotional capacity to always see where he hurt others. What he did at the time he thought was right. He realized it was wrong much later, and for him, it was too late to fix his mistakes."

"I don't care. I will never forgive him," Ubi cried.

Sybl hugged her tighter and looked up at Nafury.

"What would you have me do now?" he asked.

"You must protect Ubi. Earth is assembling a large assault with its focus on Aster. They know Asterians exist now, and their fear of us has continued to grow."

"So who are we to expect?" Nafury asked.

"The Sentry, and as the dragons are a variation of Sentry, they will use them too. Just as they used Simera despite his incredible spiritual and physical strength. Closing the Gates and Rifts won't be enough to stop them," Sybl explained. "They're already here and making a mess of the Animus Threads so that the aeri and estus energy of the Aurs don't kill them."

"So we are going to need an army, and a large one at that," Nafury concluded. "What of the dragons? Can we get them to help us before they side with Earth?"

"I don't know. I fear that they can turn the Awls against us as well."

Nafury's eyes matched hers now with that fear. Such a combined strength would be unstoppable. It was then that he remembered Xirel and how he had returned from Earth disabled and unable to speak. "What happened to Xirel..."

"I know," Sybl replied. "I don't know what to make of it."

"We have to find the one pulling all the strings, even if that means going to Earth." Nafury found himself staring at the pink flowers under their feet. This place was overly familiar beyond just his last Dream.

"This was where I first met Cirrus when I was still Asil," Sybl said.

Nafury's gaze shot back up to Sybl's. "The Dream I had—it was more a nightmare where Cirrus attacked me.

He spoke of you as well."

"This place is an exact replica of a canyon on Earth. He was just a human soldier at the time. When I found him, he was half-dead on this very field. It is true that the Chimera Mother carved this canyon in her fury against her own children. After that, however, the plumas carved it into something of my memory of Earth. I feel as if both this place and the original Cirrus is connected in some way."

"Is Hino behind this?"

"I don't know if Hino is playing a direct part in this," Sybl replied. "Either way, I don't want to assault Earth until I uncover who is behind this in the definite. Keep a close eye on Xirel, Nafury. All the Awls are connected to one another. If there is something amiss, you may be able to spot it in time from him."

"Alright."

"Is Xirel going to be okay?" Ubi asked in concern.

"I'm going to do everything I can to make sure he is," Sybl assured Ubi. "But I need your help as well. I can't affect the physical realm right now because there is no leaving Aragmoth's inner Threads alone until he has fully healed."

Ubi nodded. "Maybe my power can help, even if it only messes up their shifts."

"I'm sure it will," Sybl encouraged her. "Nafury," she said and then looked at him again, "please look after her for me. As long as there is a living Fay on Aster, and a human one for that matter, Hino's power is limited."

"You know I will. I just hope we can find out what happened to Cirrus, lest our enemies have him. If I find him and he turns out to be controlled like Simera, I don't know what I will do."

"If there is a way to cut the puppeteers strings, then Cirrus may lead you to the answer on how it can be done. I will search for him and the answers we need as well."

Nafury nodded and then rubbed his side as it felt like someone kicked him.

Sybl smiled. "Wake up now, as Xirel is about to have a fit with how lazy you are both being."

I will miss you, sister. Nafury thought as her image vanished on his waking. He had been woken up from being kicked in the side. He let the haze fade from his eyes for a moment, before looking to his shoulder that Ubi had fallen asleep on. He dared to look up at Xirel at that.

"So it wasn't just a dread feeling triggered by the past I was feeling," Xirel said.

"You saw her too?" Nafury asked as his surroundings came into focus.

"A little. With how your thoughts have suddenly included a great deal of my well-being, I can only guess what she said to you. I have felt something wrong since before I left to Earth, but I wasn't sure what it was."

"Then you're staying here with Loki. Me and Ubi can

handle the dragons."

"No, you will need an Awl to ground any other dragons that try to swarm you. Even with the power of a Fay, more than a few dragons will prove too much to handle," Xirel replied.

"I don't want you to get hurt," Ubi pleaded as she woke up and caught Xirel's hand in her own. "Please stay with the ship."

Xirel looked at Ubi for a moment, then turned away and closed his eyes. "Do you remember the day they took you from me? When I was still a Sentry?"

"Yes," Ubi replied. She lowered her eyes to the floor from the weight of the sad memory.

"I was strong enough to break free of Hino's control then and come to Aster, where I was able to live free. I fought at your mother's side the Sentry who had joined sides with Daath and defeated them. I made it to Earth and found you again, and there were no Sentry who were powerful enough to get in my way of that. Even Simera could only wound me. Whatever Hino has conjured up against us now, I will not underestimate it. Nor will I let either of you face it alone."

"But my mother said it's dangerous!" Ubi pleaded. "You said it yourself—that she was always right!"

Xirel set his other hand on the side of her face. "You worry too much for me. I can hold my own. Simera was a challenge, but they don't come stronger than him."

He looked at Nafury. "Perhaps your shift will be of great use, after all. I seriously doubt there is anything that can control Alexia aside from you."

"Yeah, I was thinking the same thing. I feel sorry for the idiot who tries just that," Nafury said as he went up onto the deck. He looked out across the water to the Torian Beach, as the ship dropped anchor. There was a single, dark blue dragon lying casually in the sand, watching them with orange eyes. Derel. "That one has gotten bigger in the last ten years," he said when Xirel and Ubi caught up to him. "With some luck, he's still the passive type." Nafury pulled the Threads of the air around him, and pulled Ubi onto his back. He lifted them off of the deck and then shifted. Making more distance from the fragile ship in a swift downburst from his wings, he flew towards the beach.

Xirel wasn't going to be left behind as he shifted and jumped the rail of the ship, landing on instead of *in* the water. He took to a run and followed them.

"He can walk on water?" Nafury said in disbelief after glancing back.

"That's so cool." On sensing Nafury's disdain, Ubi started to pet him, hoping to mend some of his ego.

FIFTEEN

Nafury hovered over the blue dragon that lay on the beach for several minutes. The smaller dragon didn't seem the least bit interested in the ship that remained some ways out. Instead, he kept his orange eyes fixated on Nafury.

Derel was Tynar and Trista's son, as well as Cecil's younger brother. He was more adventurous than many of the other young dragons, and he was also one of the more intelligent ones. There was no way to tell whether the dragon would attack them like Simera had.

Nafury looked back at Xirel as the chimera Awl turned his eyes from the sky to the waves. If Derel decided to attack them, his first move would likely be a tsunami with his command over water. He didn't know if Xirel would be able to do anything with the Thread against that kind of force.

"My brother made it clear that he wants nothing more to do with you," Derel said when Nafury landed in front of him. "You have some nerve bringing that treacherous Alexia over here as well."

"Ubi would like to see her mother's grave," Nafury replied, hoping to avoid having to try and explain anything.

Derel looked at the Fay who stayed on Nafury's back. "Yes, we all know about the Outcast Fay. She is dangerous and should not have been brought to Aster."

"Is that what Simera has told you?" Nafury asked.

"Simera? Simera was dead before I was born," Derel replied.

Nafury let out a silent breath of relief. News of Simera's more recent death hadn't spread to here, yet. "So who else is going on about how dangerous she is, then?"

Derel looked at Ubi as if for the answer. "Her story is in the Texts."

"Let me guess, these books have suddenly appeared? How peculiar. Look, I would like to discuss your schooling all day, but I have other things to attend to. My niece and I are going to visit my sister's grave, right now. I trust there won't be any problems with the merchants?"

Derel looked at Xirel who had turned his gaze from the skies to give him a cold stare. "I won't bother them, but I make no promises with what the others will do. Derel was on his feet now, making his way backwards before he took to the air. Nafury did the same some moments later.

"It's so pretty," Ubi said as she looked at the crystal-like castle rise in the distance. From its center, a pinkish-purple glow rose into the atmosphere and spread across it. "It looks like from a fairy tale."

Nafury laughed. "We will get a closer look later on. Let's go do what I said we would, first." He turned his wings in the direction of the Bedlam Waterway.

Ubi looked back to where they left Xirel.

The Awl nodded in her direction and thought to her, *'I will hold the beach until you get back. Be safe.'*

After a twenty minute flight, they reached the Bedlam Waterway. Nafury floated down through the mists to a ledge and gave a quick look for danger. Satisfied, he unshifted and lowered Ubi down from his back. They headed inside the small cave that was near the waterfall that fed the river. Some ways inside, they found Sybl's and Cirrus' gravestones. Just to the side stood Serena's as well. A small, intricately carved shrine had been built within the cavern that hadn't been there last time he was here.

"Who did this?" Ubi asked, looking all around before going over to her mother's grave. Fresh, pink flowers from the Casus Beli Canyon lay on Sybl's marker.

"It's not much, but it was something to do with my past time," a voice said from behind a pillar. A dragoon with short, blue hair and orange, blind eyes stepped out. He didn't have Derel's better looks, but Cecil was always known more for his brains. "What are you doing here, Nafury?" Cecil asked.

"Is it so wrong to see if my former kind are doing well?" Nafury replied.

"We've been just fine with your Apocalypse attempt out of the way. And I see you found yourself another Fay."

Ubi started to quickly lose patience with the arrogant dragoon. Nafury could feel her willing herself to not make Cecil's blue dragon shift eat him.

"Do you intend to kill this one as well?" Cecil asked in an attempt to spite him.

Nafury lost his cool, and launched himself at Cecil. But the dragoon was ready for his hit, and caught the punch aimed for his face. "You already know that was out of my control."

"Yet what is done is done and you were the one to kill her. I suppose it was inevitable, as you always were a monster. Funny how we've gone from sparring with each other as children to fighting in adulthood. You never did grow up," Cecil mocked.

The next strike didn't come from Nafury. A rush of estus energy surged from Ubi's hands and threw Cecil across the shrine. The dragoon hit the cave wall with a vengeance, sending rocks and dirt falling to the ground around him.

"You are the monster for speaking like that!" Ubi shouted as she looked down at Cecil, her eyes a flashing a bright blue. "My mother has forgiven him. I have forgiven him. You are the only child here who refuses to grow up! The world is more than just dragons and pretty flowers!"

Cecil wiped away some of the blood from the back of his head and slowly got to his feet. "And that would definitely be Sybl's temper. I might have had more faith in you if you looked like your mother and inherited your father's demeanour."

Nafury caught Ubi's arms before she could claw Cecil apart. "Easy there, he's not worth it." He had to use all of his and Alexia's strength to hold Ubi back, as she was incredibly strong when angry. "Ubi, calm down. This is what he wants—an excuse to get rid of us."

Ubi calmed down somewhat and Nafury let go of her. "I won't be able to sleep at night with the thought of this animal near my mother's grave." She looked around for Cecil's shift, but it was hiding well.

"We also came here to warn you of Earth's latest threat coming for Aster," Nafury said to Cecil.

"Hino is neutralized. Sybl's death saw to that," Cecil replied. "And the Sentry can't survive on Aster as long as the Soph and Atrum's Aurs are up. If any humans venture to Aster, then they won't get far. So exactly what are we defending against?"

"Sybl thinks this is something else. Something even more dangerous," Nafury replied. "Anything and anyone who can link back to the Sentry, descendants of Solar, the Awls, and even the chimera may become a threat."

"And just when did you speak with her? She's in the realm of death."

"Let's just say I found out what happens when two Dreamwalkers Dream the same thing. Look, Cecil, I hate you. I think I have always hated you as much as you have me, but don't be blinded stupid by that fact. From what I gathered all these years is that my sister has never been wrong. Bring up Toria's defences and do what the position you've taken up for yourself requires of you."

"Why doesn't the whole planet just attack us?" Cecil replied, talking mostly to himself. "What exactly has the power to control that kind of a force?"

"I'm still looking for it. But I have seen that it exists. Xirel was almost overtaken with it. Then I had to kill Simera shortly after he followed the Awl leader back to Aster, at the Sanctus," Nafury replied.

Cecil's pale eyes turned skeptical. "I won't believe that. Even with Alexia as your shift, Simera was unbeatable."

Nafury unsheathed his blade and threw it at the dragoon's feet. It wasn't his blade that he had in his sheathe, but Simera's. He figured that Alexia must have taken it from the dragoon's body after killing him. "Believe that then, or don't. I don't care. I'm leaving now. This isn't my home anymore—it never really was." He turned and started to leave then, and Ubi followed behind.

Nafury reached the outside ledge and started to shift, before Ubi caught his arm and stopped him. He read her eyes and lifted her chin up. "Don't let him get to you. Cecil has always been a creep."

"I don't want to see Toria anymore," she said and absentmindedly looked him over. She wanted to sleep in his shift for their return and she didn't know how to manipulate him in such a manner to activate it. "This place makes me sad and I don't like any of it."

"It could be the Aur," Nafury said, offering her the excuse when he knew exactly what was bothering her now. "A dark Fay would be more comfortable near the Atrum's Aur. I'm sorry then that we won't see your castle up close."

Ubi shook her head. "It's fine."

He pulled her close and into his shift with his best effort to douse her sadness with sleep. Then Nafury stepped off of the ledge, and spread his wings in the direction of the Torian beach.

On returning to the beach, he landed next to Xirel. The Awl hadn't had any visitors to deal with in their absence. The merchants were quickly finishing their gatherings as well. They would be ready to start the return to the Suzerain Continent by nightfall.

"Anything?" Nafury asked.

"I'm not sure. The Threads have changed on this side of the world. Is Ubi alright?" Xirel asked.

"Cecil pissed her off, but other than a bit sad, she's alright."

"Did he listen to you?" Xirel asked.

"I don't know. I don't plan on hanging around to find out if he did or not, either."

"The silence here worries me. That and can you feel that in the air?"

Nafury tilted his head, as he tried to tune into the Threads that bothered Xirel. "That is weird. What is it?"

"Someone is realigning the Thread, and I don't think it will be in our favour. We should hasten our return to the Suzerain Continent."

'It's electricity,' Alexia voiced to Nafury by psi. 'They're statically charging the Thread.'

"Oh no," Nafury said.

"What?" Xirel asked, concerned.

"Alexia says it's electricity."

"And there are no thunderstorms on

Aster..." Xirel brought his fingers to his mouth and let out a sharp whistle. It was the emergency signal that they were all leaving, right now.

The captain began to shout orders and his crew began to move at double speed. They loaded everything they could carry last moment onto the small boats for the GLORIA. In fifteen minutes, the last phelan shifters and humans were off of the beach and paddling for the ship.

Nafury spotted the enemy first within the trees. "A Sentry, there."

Xirel looked in the direction that he did and unsheathed his blade. "Go for the legs, it's their weak point.

Cries of fear could be heard from the GLORIA. Several of the sailors had spotted the semi-transparent, insect-like creature in the trees as well.

"Is it alone?" Nafury asked. When he got no answer from Xirel, he took to the air and then landed right on top of the creature. It screamed and thrashed, and one of its bladed arms cut the side of his face. Nafury pinned it down, before sending his teeth for its neck. It died, leaving nothing but silver ash in his claws. He looked around if any more would join the fight, but only silence answered. The answer was too easy, and he focused harder. He sensed one moving invisibly for Xirel, and he launched himself back into the air. He came down on the Sentry just as the Awl cut the Threads to its legs from under it. "Xirel!"

"Yes, I see them," the Awl replied and looked to the next closest one. "They can still reach the ship. We must hold them off a little longer."

Nafury charged at the one Xirel saw and crippled it with several rakes from his claws. Another came up from behind him and Xirel collapsed its legs. That gave Nafury time to react and turn around to kill the creature.

Xirel took focus on the next Sentry to come for him, and swiftly cut it down with a swipe of his sword. He paused for a moment then as the Sentry all vanished from sight again. One landed a bladed scythe arm across his back and he stumbled forward. He fell to one knee as it came back and nearly took his head off. Now frantic, he looked around for his attacker, but they remained completely invisible. "Nafury!"

Nafury pushed away another Sentry that was on him, and looked to Xirel. He took to the air and then swiftly scooped up Xirel as if he were prey. A heartbeat later, the Sentry dropped its scythe-like forearm where the Awl had been. "That one is a problem."

"Indeed," Xirel replied. The Awl was content to dangle between the dragon's claws out of harms way. "Thank you."

"Ubi would send me into the next life in pieces if you died. So that's not going to happen. The fantasy cruise is over—we're leaving," Nafury said and turned in the air to follow the GLORIA. He hoped that the Sentry hadn't learned how to swim or fly.

SIXTEEN

Ubi woke to the feeling of someone on her feet. She sat up in bed in the cabin given to her on the GLORIA, and found Loki asleep on her feet. Only Awls weren't supposed to need sleep. "Loki?"

He looked up at her and pulled his arms away from where he had been resting. "Sorry, Princess. I was just worried about you."

"I'm alright."

"I know, but it was a close one on the beach. The Sentry shouldn't be able to move around on Aster like that. They can't survive the aeri and estus energies anymore than we can sunlight. Or at least, they couldn't before. Everything is just all wrong."

"We'll figure it out, Loki. Worrying non-stop won't help. Why don't we change the subject. You're supposed to be some kind of renowned storyteller, aren't you?"

Loki returned a small smile as he accepted the change of topic. "What story would the Princess like to hear?"

"If you told my mother a story, I want to hear the same one, just like you told her."

Loki's expression turned into that of surprise. "Alright." He sat down on the bed next to her. She lay back down and he pulled the blanket higher over her. "Once upon a time there was a beautiful world where everyone was born as twins. No one was ever born alone or without someone to love. They called the firstborn the Mei, and the second to be born, the Aliyr. The Mei was considered the shield into the world, and the Aliyr the sword. As such, the female was almost always the shield and the male, the sword.

"But there were exceptions. Asteria was unlike all the others of her kind, and was born alone. They called her a Sylph, which were considered to be gods as they were able to survive entirely alone. She wielded great power and wisdom despite that. As she made the world flourish in prosperity and peace, they named it after her; Aster. But this did not mean she wished to be alone, so when a Sentry of Earth fell in love with her, she agreed to be his wife.

"Daath gave her a beautiful Unicorn on her wedding night. In its horn, he had Threaded the names of all 3000 Eminor loyal to him. From its horn that was also a curved, bladed staff called a festra, she could command the dark army as she pleased. He in turn, would have her to please him. But the army's primary purpose on Aster was to devour and destroy any nightmares to come near her. They became known as the 'Nightmare Eaters.'

"It was a world of peace, so the Eminor lived peacefully alongside the Asterians. They aided them with their powers in exchange for their life energies. When they were unneeded, they would sleep peacefully entertained by the Asterian's few nightmares.

"There was no hunger, suffering, pain or disease. The Asterians could wield the spirits like magic. They could cure and build almost everything, limited only by their imaginations. Every once in a while, they would stir up Earth's humans for inspiration. They would indirectly inspire their love for each other, even where it caused war. There was no need for their own kind to wage war, for they had the power of psi. They could see into the minds and feelings of those around them. Where a dispute lay, it was settled by the power of their own spirits.

"The most powerful Dreamer would always intimidate the other to yield. Then the conflict would be settled. Or the opposition's spirits would be devoured. In such case, the host was exiled to continue their pursuit of misery on Earth. Many became or returned to being Sentries.

"Asteria and Daath had a baby girl and boy, twins which they named Asil and Erebus. Unlike most twins,

Asil was born as the Aliyr, and Erebus the Mei. They lived happy for a time. There was nothing that existed that could match Asil's beauty or Erebus' strength. The people took their love for one another as an example to live their own lives in balance. They were the first Fay; fairy immortals composed of two worlds.

"But the happiness was not to last. The Sentries from Earth formed together to take Daath back, and the army that he had fled Earth with. They feared that the child Prince and Princess would amass a force against them. As such, their very existence was a threat. But the Asterians were masters of the energies of life and death, aeri and estus alike. So they had to create a weapon capable of wielding and defending against both.

"So they drowned the evil and good from Earth, and fused both energies together. Of the storm that erupted over the flood waters was born the Dragon Moon.

"They unleashed the dragon's rage on Aster, and it destroyed everything. Asteria's and Daath's combined energies were not enough to stop the monster. Before they died, they were able to tear the wings from the Dragon Moon.

"So Erebus and Asil fell from the highest heavens in the universe. The Dragon Moon pursued them, slowed by its loss of wings. Yet it was determined to destroy what was the last of the existence of Aster. He caught Erebus and devoured him. He caught up to Asil as well. But before he could attack her, she unravelled the Threads that were on her mother's festra. Then she sung the names of the Eminor within.

"The Eminor, immune to death as they were, combined around her. They created a dragon even larger than the Dragon Moon. It could bend the folds of space into black holes like a whirlpool in an ocean. Aragmoth attacked and consumed the Dragon Moon, fueled by Asil's rage and sadness. It hurled its soul back to Earth, taking the estus energy from the Dragon Moon into itself. Of the titan's bones, Aragmoth left them to forever float in space near the Earth as its moon. A testament and warning of his power should the Sentries ever try and cross him again."

"Are there any stories of me?" Ubi asked, hopeful.

"Hmmm," Loki said as he closed his eyes, and tapped into the Threads that connected him to all the other Awls. "Xirel is the only one who remembers one of your previous lives. Kas likely erased all memory of you. That or those who would remember you were destroyed by the Dragon Moon. None of the other Sentry who have fallen seem to have memories of you, either."

"I will never forgive my father," Ubi said and turned away from him and to her side. "It's one thing to die, but to be erased from existence entirely?"

Loki set a hand on her shoulder, willing her not to cry.

"How did you die, Loki?"

Loki was momentarily stunned by her question that came with no consideration to his feelings. "I drowned when Tenu and the Phoenix took out Mer City. I couldn't make it to the surface in time."

"And your Sentry? Why did it fall to Aster?" Ubi asked.

"I'm not sure. It won't tell me."

Ubi turned back around and looked at him. Then she reached out her hand and touched his face.

Loki felt weird and looked down to see that she was unravelling the illusion weave he had around him. "No, wait—" He looked back at her, as only his pitch black, hairless humanoid-like form now remained. It was what Awls truly looked like on Aster. He now looked as terrifying as a demon. But she wasn't scared.

"I knew it was Xirel who came for me on Earth cause I could see his last memories as a Sentry when he touched me. Those memories are an important piece of you and should be seen."

"I... I don't want to make you sad, Princess," Loki said, and calmed down despite his current state.

"The saddest stories sometimes have the happiest endings," she said. "But if you never try and get through the sadness, you can never reach that happy ending."

Loki didn't resist her as she looked into his mind. Images of Earth flashed by him, until they slowed to one. In this memory he was hunting something, he realized. He was on a bridge on a bright, summer day. It was warm and humid. He was also three times bigger than anything around him. The vehicles passed through and under him like he wasn't there at all. Loki soon saw what he hunted, but he was out of reach of it. The demonic shadow struck the bridge hard enough to make it crack, then threw a large yellow bus over the side.

Loki ran to it and reached out for the bus, but it was too late. The vehicle hit the water from a terrible height. The screams of the children inside were drowned in its depths within moments. Loki came back to the present just as a surge of pain burned through him.

Ubi was holding herself partly up on an elbow now, wiping the tears out of his eyes.

"Ubi..." Loki said, trying to get a grip of himself. By defensive reflex, his illusion weave had already begun to restore itself.

"That's why you came to Aster and took so long to find a host. You wanted someone strong, and with a similar past so that this one could hide behind it unnoticed. You found that."

"Did I?" Loki asked, unsure of himself. He had disillusioned himself into thinking that he was stronger now. Little of him felt like he actually was.

"But you're happy now, I can feel it. Nafury and Xirel make you feel less lonely, and you're important to your Tribe. That's what's important, isn't it?"

Loki caught her hand, then nodded. "I suppose for the most part I am. The question is though, are you? Will you ever tell Nafury and Xirel the truth?"

Ubi pulled her hand away and lay back down, then stared at the ceiling. She knew that he had seen her thoughts, just as clearly as she had seen his. The psi memory trip worked both ways. "I'm like you right now. I need to keep disillusioning myself until I believe it. Fake it until you make it, or in my case, become it."

"Is that a saying on Earth?" Loki asked.

Ubi nodded. "I will tell them—I just can't tell them now."

"Alright," Loki said and got to his feet. "But I'll agree to this only because I believe you can be happy if you try. Promise me that you won't let me down."

"I promise," Ubi replied.

"Then let's leave it at that," he said and headed for the door. "Goodnight, Princess, and thank you."

"Goodnight, Master Hunter."

Loki closed the door as he thought about the name she had just given him. His last memory was of failure, but there were many more that had not been. His Sentry half just got tired of being on the front lines of so many tragedies. Even now, Loki instinctively kept his distance from conflict. It wasn't that he was scared of it, it was because he had witnessed enough lifetimes filled with pain.

"Is she alright?" Nafury asked, stopping before Loki.

"She's fine." Loki returned his thoughts to the present and looked up at Nafury. "She just fell asleep right now." He left for the deck at that.

Nafury double checked by psi on Ubi, and saw that she was indeed asleep. Then he turned his focus back on Loki who was acting unusual.

SEVENTEEN

Kenshe didn't know that he still had it in him to be so brilliant. He had reached a new record with feeling completely full of himself. His plan to get near Ubi was ingenious. It was the same tactic that he had used to get close to her mother. How fitting, he thought, that it would work on her daughter.

The chimera around him paid him little mind, and he kept a perfect cool as he pretended to blend in. Even when a large ball hit him in the head. Even when a bowl of water was flung at him, complete with bits of meat. Even when one of the plumas sunk their teeth into his fluffy, grizzled brown tail...and didn't let up.

Kenshe clenched his phelan teeth together and slowly turned to look at the winged kitten. A warning flash from his red eyes put out the bright green eyes of his attacker all at once. The small pluma let go of him, before running off with a small cry.

"Aw, did the kitty bite you?" Ubi said as she walked over to the True pup and lifted him up from under his shoulders. "Silly kitties."

Kenshe couldn't have asked for more luck. He was literally purring from it which helped with his act to put his best cute forward. He had her right where he wanted. All he had to do now was—

"Ubi, what are you doing?" Nafury asked from the doorway to the nursery.

Ubi turned around and lifted the True closer for him to see. "Isn't he adorable? I was going to die from the cute overload in this room alone. I can't believe he can purr!" she said and hugged it. "It's like he's half cat!"

Nafury lifted an eyebrow as he studied the True pup. He hadn't see one in centuries. He could only gather that they were impossible to see being what they were. Anything stupid enough to trip past a mother True phelan would have been dead. Instantly. "Eh, yeah. Sort of. But he stinks. You should think about giving him a bath."

Ubi sniffed the pup's head. "He doesn't stink. He doesn't smell like anything."

"Maybe it's what he ate then," Nafury said and looked around at the chimera nursery. All sorts of combinations of animals were around him. Some had already been possessed by fallen Sentry and had become Awls. They stood out as the more mature, less trouble making of the lot. He thought that it must feel odd to have their mature minds fused into such small bodies, but it wasn't his business. If Xirel didn't alarm to their presence, he wasn't going to start something. "Are you sure they're all accounted for?" he teased.

"Seriously, uncle? He didn't eat any."

Nafury smiled and shook his head. "Don't be too long. Xirel is enjoying tormenting me by keeping me out of his conversation with Loki. I'm getting bored from being out of the loop. I need you as an excuse to get back in it." They had returned to the Efereal Mountains after their horror cruise to the Torian Continent. Their fear was that it would get hit next, while it was still recovering from Kenshe's attack. Despite being in a mountain of Awls and chimera, Nafury still felt vulnerable.

"Alright," Ubi replied and watched him go. She turned her focus back on the True in her arms and smelled him again. "We might as well give you a bath just in case I'm nose-blind or something..." She carried him over to a large bowl and sat him down in the icy water. Finding a brush, she started to scrub him down.

Kenshe's mission could wait, as the full body scrub he was getting was just too enjoyable to turn down. He struggled to keep his focus and his size for that matter through the whole bath. When she was done, he was left half-tranced from bliss as she wrapped him in a wool blanket.

"Ow!" Ubi squeaked.

Kenshe's giant ears perked up, as he hadn't bitten her, yet. They simultaneously looked down to see where a kitten's claws had raked her calf. The pluma had scratched her hard enough to make her bleed.

"That wasn't very nice!" she said and crouched down to shoo away her attacker with her hand.

Kenshe jumped out of her arms and quickly played the hero, gently licking her wound. Luck favoured him today, as he wouldn't have to bite her, after all.

"Ew...okay, that's great," Ubi said and picked him back up. She wrapped him back in the blanket and left the nursery.

Every breath Kenshe took now was focused on keeping his form small. Her endless memories raced through his head with no sign of slowing down. Sybl's blood had been an intense heat, but Ubi's was a blistering cold that stabbed at his inner veins. He could take the pain, as he had anticipated it. Her soul was much older than he originally calculated. Easily as old as his own soul as his mind worked fast to sort out the images he recognized of the first Aster. Of the Dragon Moon's attack on it. Then the timeline pushed forward and he saw her last dozen lives, and how she was murdered. Her rage and hate was insatiable and wasn't limited to just Earth. He didn't know how she had built such a solid concrete wall around all of it, but she was no novice with psi Thread. She was very likely the most masterful deceiver he had ever seen.

Ubi set him down on the bed in her room. He pulled his mind back to the present as he watched her like he would watch an adversary. Nafury and Xirel hadn't the slightest idea what they were dealing with. A very large piece of the enemy they searched for was right in here. Her very blood was what was poisoning the Awls and dragons into becoming puppets. They could have only taken that from her when she was on Earth. What angered him is that she knew this already. The only thing she didn't seem to know was who was behind it.

He didn't look away as she changed into a clean, cream tunic and pants. It was awkward to watch her as she looked just like a female Kas might. The scars on her pale body were real. She had been a prisoner and test subject through this incarnation. He would have felt sorry for her if she had any kind of real emotion in her to justify her as a person, let alone a Fay.

Nafury had sealed his own doom. Ubi felt little for him aside from using him as an extra shield to hide who she truly was. He could feel her attraction for Xirel, but he doubted that would last long once her true self showed its face. Either way, Kenshe had got what he wanted and didn't care about the rest of her story. This Fay was lost, and he had enough of his own problems. He stood up to leave, before stopping when Nafury appeared in the doorway again. *Curses! Go away you infernal bastard!*

"I'm ready, let's go," Ubi said and picked up the True to take with her to show to Xirel.

"You're still carrying that mutt around?" Nafury sighed.

"I gave him a bath," she said in the pup's defense. "See, smell." She lifted him to Nafury's face.

"I'll take your word for it," Nafury replied as he leaned away from the pup. They continued walking for Xirel's makeshift throne room.

While being carried like a stuffed toy, Kenshe pondered all the consequences of biting Nafury's useless head off right now.

EIGHTEEN

Nafury stopped in the hallway leading to the cavern where Xirel was. A glimmer of gold had caught his attention. When he looked closer, he saw that the object lying on the floor of the connecting hallway looked a lot like his helmet.

"Nafury?" Ubi said.

"Go on ahead, Ubi. I think one of the chimera found my helmet for me."

Ubi briefly glanced at what he was looking at, before nodding and heading the rest of the way on her own. She pushed open one of the two heavy wooden doors and went inside. Xirel was sitting on a higher, intricately carved wooden chair. Loki was also there and sat before him. They both stopped conversing to acknowledge her arrival.

"Princess," Loki greeted.

"You're not back to talk about sailing over to dragon island again I hope?"

"No," Loki replied and finished with a laugh. "We were actually just talking about you and how to go about training you to learn Thread."

Ubi sat next to Loki with her pup and looked at Xirel. "Here I was worried about that too, as I didn't catch any fish..."

"Xirel," Loki playfully scolded him. "That was rather mean."

"It was one of my few attempts at humour," Xirel said and leaned his cheek against his hand. "I've learned my lesson. It won't happen again." He sounded like a child who had just been reprimanded.

Ubi smiled at him, and Xirel seemed to cheer up a bit when he returned it.

"Soooo," Loki said, interrupting their staring, "we've taken to adopting stray True pups now? I didn't think they ever strayed..."

"He was being tormented by the other babies in the nursery. I felt bad for him, so I took him with me," Ubi said.

"Loki here is much like your True pup that you carry," Xirel started, shifting to lean back in his seat.

"Oh?" Ubi asked, interested. "Come to think of it, you do seem rather young to have known my mother..."

"Heh, that's because Awls don't physically age." Loki

pulled off his silver mask, and then looked her straight in the eyes.

The light green stars over his eyes were still there, and just as neat to look at. His orange eyes conveyed to her that he intended to keep her secret from Xirel, but she would have to play his game in return.

Loki smiled and looked away from her. "Do I look like a human from your world, Ubi?"

"Some contacts for your eyes and maybe a bit of hair dye and you'd be set. You have the most interesting birthmark ever, and I don't think I could bring myself to put makeup over it." Ubi leaned closer for a better look at him. "What did my mother think of you?"

Loki's smile grew wider. "She got mad at me when I refused to take off my mask. When she hit it off by accident, she got even madder. Sybl didn't take well to anyone thinking that she was shallow." Loki's smile faded from another memory of sadness, and he took the mask in both his hands and began to manipulate it with his power over fire. "When is your birthday, Princess?"

"Uh, February fourteenth. I only remember my human one," she replied.

"Valentines Day, interesting. Earth's designated day to show your significant other how much you love them. How fitting." His fire grew hotter and larger, until the silver mask took the shape of a slender dragon. In the figurine's hands, it held a large heart-shaped card. He made sure it was cool before handing it to her. "I'm sorry I missed your birthday by over a month."

Ubi smiled and shook her head. "There are like none of Earth's customs here. You don't have to apologize."

"On the contrary, you are here, which means all of Earth's customs and celebrations are now as well," Loki replied. "Most of them are rather fun. Knowledge of both worlds is important to Awls. That's why despite being a nobody when I was a dragoon, I was chosen to lead the Eastern Tribes on becoming an Awl. My mother may have died when I was still young, but she left me one of the greatest gifts in the eyes of Awls."

"Oh?" Ubi asked, curious to what the rest of his story was.

"My never-ending curiosity and creativity."

The True's ears perked higher.

"Yet Xirel is the chimera's chief leader, right?" Ubi asked.

"Yes, Ubi, but my time is coming to an end," Xirel explained. "I think that Loki would be the best choice for taking my place."

"I don't understand—you look fine," Ubi said in concern.

"Sentry Awls can live for thousands of years, sometimes even more like Alexia. But eventually their energy gives out," Loki added. "Do not worry, though, Ubi. He still has a good hundred years at the absolute least in him. We just have to think of the future."

Ubi didn't reply, as her heart filled with even more worry for Xirel's wellbeing.

"Putting that aside for now, we want to help train you to use Thread," Xirel said. "But a great deal of your mind is sealed off by someone more than a beginner with it. At first, we thought it might be another psi, possibly even Nafury, but we're not so sure anymore."

"I don't understand," Ubi said, playing innocent.

Loki looked for a moment at Xirel, before looking back at her. "We want to do everything we can to have your trust. You are important to us because you are a Fay and you're Sybl's daughter."

"That and I also care for you beyond those reasons alone," Xirel added. "I am certain that I never stopped caring about you since we first met on Earth in our other lifetime."

Ubi blushed, and she unconsciously squeezed her True phelan till it squeaked.

"It's not like age is a problem," Loki said, lightening the air around them. "Technically, you're older than all of us combined." He finished with a wide smile.

"I guess you're right," Ubi said, while trying to rub the blush out of her cheeks.

"You don't have to say anything in return," Xirel said. "I won't sit here and pretend to understand all of what you've been through. Nor will I ever force you to reveal your feelings about me. I just thought that it was important to be made known." He leaned forward and pulled himself to his feet then, and walked over to the exit.

Loki took the True from Ubi, and she got up and went over to Xirel.

"Your uncle sure is taking his time. What is he doing?" Xirel asked, feeling that a change of subject was in order. "At the very least he could respond to my psi."

"He saw his helmet and thinks a chimera returned it. It sounded important to him," Ubi said.

"His helmet? The one that Feryl took?" Xirel said with a serious tone. Immediately he looked at the True that Loki was holding. "Kenshe."

Kenshe returned a smile of all teeth, before Loki stood up and threw the pup against a wall. The phelan scrambled back to his feet and shook the hit off, before shifting into his human appearance in a rush of brown and grey mist. "You really are getting old, Xirel."

Xirel answered by unsheathing his blade as Loki did the same with his daggers. "What do you want?"

"He wants to die," Ubi said, furious from being duped by the phelan shifter. She looked for Kenshe's shift, and forced her will on it to attack him. Only the phelan spirit didn't respond to her power. "Why isn't...my power working?"

Kenshe's smile grew wider when the effects of having

tasted her blood proved to have bonuses. "I just stopped by to say hi, but if you want a fight," he said, unsheathing his own blade. Then he grabbed several Threads leading to Loki and Xirel. "Mind you, the full body bath was really nice."

Ubi's fury with him rose another level.

"You have spilled enough blood in my home. There is the door," Xirel said, walking away from it, as he pulled Ubi behind him.

They all stopped in their tracks when the mountain shook all around them.

"What was that?" Loki asked, as he tried to get a reading from the Threads, as Xirel kept hold of Kenshe's lifelines.

The shrilling cry from a dragon echoed through the halls of the mountain.

"I swear if he's gone berserk again...!" Xirel said.

Kenshe knew he was high up on the dragon's hit list and would die if he remained cornered. It was then that he noticed the wall move from behind Xirel. "Xirel, LOOK OUT!"

Xirel spun around on sensing what he saw too late. He pulled Ubi out of harms way as a scythe-like arm cut through the air and hit his sword arm instead of landing on her. His blade dropped to the floor, and he stumbled backwards. The Sentry gave him no time to change the Threads he was holding.

The Sentry lifted its arm to attack again, and Loki disabled its Threads. The monster cried out in pain and lifted its other arm to strike.

Kenshe was now in his larger shifted form, and launched himself at it, landing his teeth in the Sentry's neck.

The Sentry thrashed around violently, screaming as it tried to throw Kenshe from it. Its own blood was betraying its invisibility. Finally, it suffocated, and Kenshe dropped it, where it shortly after turned into stardust. He backed away to catch his breath.

Ubi looked at Loki as he went over to Xirel and started to heal his arm.

"We have to get out of the mountain. There's no room to fight in here," Loki said, trying to remain calm.

They pulled Xirel to his feet just as another cry from the White Death went out. They ran for the exit to the cavern, but just before they could reach it, it collapsed as the mountain shook again. They were now sealed inside.

"Dammit," Loki said and looked for another way out. There were no other exits or any windows to the room. Then he looked at Kenshe as his hand was bleeding. The phelan shifter touched the stone floor, forming a Rift to the Keol. "How can you do that? There has to be a thousand tons of stone between us and the bottom of this mountain."

"It only works one way," Kenshe replied. "You

coming?"

Loki gulped and looked at Xirel. "The Keol will kill us instantly."

"Yeah, I figured that. Best of luck then," Kenshe said with an insincere tone. He looked up as several stone slabs dislodged from the ceiling. He stepped out of the way to avoid being crushed, and they broke into hundreds of pieces on hitting the ground.

"You have to go with him," Xirel said, and pulled away from Ubi. "The Keol won't effect you like it does us with your estus energy to protect you."

"I'm not leaving you," she pleaded, and held tightly onto his arm.

"Loki and I can get out of here, but outside are the Sentry. You will be safe in the Keol. Please, Ubi. They are after you. They may even call off the attack entirely with you absent."

"Let's go, brat," Kenshe said and grabbed Ubi's arm like she were a doll and dragged her to the Rift.

Ubi kicked and screamed as she tried to break free of his grip, but it was no use. The phelan shifter was as strong as she was.

"Kenshe, if you harm her — !" Xirel warned.

"Relax, she's no longer a threat to me and I have no taste for killing females." He threw her into the dark puddle of the Rift, which she fell through and into the Keol. "If you live, you can come and pick her up at the

Atrum. She's likely to try my patience rather fast, so don't take too long." At that, Kenshe entered the Rift after her.

Kenshe emerged in the Keol to find Ubi pacing about as her feet burned from the hot, solid lava under her. He leaned down and touched the ground with his estus energy, cooling it down. After a few moments she stopped pacing.

"Let me out of here! I'm not going anywhere with you!" Ubi shouted at him.

"Good, cause I had no intention to take you back to the Atrum. Despite the fact that you almost killed me, I honestly wanted to give you the benefit of the doubt. I wanted to believe that you were Sybl's daughter and that you had a reason to be alive and on Aster for that matter. I even doubted my best friend. I thought that maybe for the first time in all of Kas' incarnations that he actually made a mistake. I mean, banish his own daughter? Who does that? Heck, 'monster' is an overused term on Aster if anything. But now I get it. I understand why I had to watch Kas slowly die inside every single day. He withered away, unable to touch his own soultwin without being crippled inside. All the reasons to why he had to suffer lead back to you."

"Stop it!" Ubi screamed at him. "You don't know anything!"

"No, no, I don't think so. You see, where you cross my line of no return is your feelings for your mother. I watched her suffer through so much pain and like you, a lifetime of being unwanted. Despite that she still gave the last of herself to keep us all here and alive today. You are a selfish bitch to think that you are the only one in the whole universe who has suffered!" Kenshe shouted at her.

Ubi fell to her knees, sobbing. "Stop...it!"

"Well, you've sealed your own Fate. I hate Nafury, but at the same time I feel sorry for him for when he does find out what you've been hiding. If there is any mercy left in Aragmoth, he will die here and today."

"He can't find out!" Ubi pleaded. "Please, stop this! What do you want? I... I can go with you. Surely a Fay is still of use to you?"

"I don't want you. You quite frankly disgust me. No, I'm going to leave you right here in this hellish desert where you belong. Aragmoth can deal with you if he wants. But do yourself a favour and don't call for Nafury's help when he wakes up from his berserked state. Let him think you're dead—I know you're much better with psi Thread than you've been letting on. Because I've seen what Nafury turns into when furious, both as Damek and with Cirrus. I seriously doubt that your mother would intervene when Nafury tears your heart out. She was never a fool." Kenshe shifted into his phelan form at that and turned to leave.

"No, wait!" Ubi screamed and ran towards him. Only it was too late as he took off without hesitation, leaving a flurry of black ashes behind him.

Ubi let her cries vibrate through all Aragmoth's Threads around her as she called for help. She didn't want to die forgotten in such a hell. Something answered her, and she looked ahead as a phelan appeared. At first she thought it was Kenshe, until she could see that its fur was a deep black and not a grizzled brown.

It walked closer to her and she stood at the ready, not knowing what it would do. It said nothing as it crouched down before her, offering her a lift.

Ubi calculated her options, then took the phelan shifter's offer and climbed onto his back. It turned and then started at a quick run.

Kenshe returned to where he had left Ubi, but found no trace of her. Whatever had found her didn't leave a Thread of scent behind that he could follow. He reached out his psi to her, but a surge of pain struck him back. Fear began to swell up in him of just what had caused her to vanish into thin air.

NINETEEN

They were waiting for something, and she had no idea what. Ubi watched the phelan shifters around her carefully, as they did the same with her. No one said anything, as they continued to talk to only each other by psi. Her phelan shifter rescuer had brought her here, to a cave under a large cliff. They were some ways from the Atrum as only its dark Aur could be seen hitting the atmosphere in the distance. She looked at her rescuer as he brought a bowl of soup from the pot at the center of their camp to her. With every inch of her starved, she took it and thanked him. "Where have you brought me?"

"This is our camp," were the first words she heard from him. "Right now you're about twenty miles from Atrum City." He sat down a comfortable distance in front of her, all the while keeping his eyes locked with hers. He was a young shifter, as his red eyes still glowed bright with energy and he had no scars. His long, black hair fell to his waist, and looked like it hadn't been brushed for a while. "What's your name?"

"Ubi," she replied, between spoonfuls of her soup.

"I'm Terren," he replied. "You seem rather lost. Do you belong to anyone?"

Ubi set the empty bowl down on the ground after a few minutes and shook her head. She looked to the cave some meters away as an old woman appeared from within it. Her hair draped her in silver, and her red eyes were cloudy. Her clothes, drapes of dark fabric, were long due for repairs. The ayame looked older than everyone she had ever met, combined.

"This one is special, Terren," the old ayame said, walking closer to them. "You must not speak to her as if she were a mere commoner."

Terren looked at the ayame and nodded, before looking back at Ubi. "Her energy is unlike anything I've ever seen. Who is she, Mother?"

"She is the dark Fay—daughter of Erebus and Asil," the old ayame said. Any and all whispers, aloud and by psi stopped within the Pack as all eyes focused on Ubi. "I do not understand why such a precious one as yourself would have been left alone in the Keol."

"The Sentry attacked the Efereal Mountains. Kenshe helped me get out, but then left me behind," Ubi explained.

"Kenshe?" the Mother Weaver said. "He would defy the caels directly by abandoning you in the Keol?"

"Well, that may prove a problem if he changes his mind," Terren added.

"I'm not going anywhere with him. He left my friends to die in the Efereal Mountains," Ubi said bitterly.

"Who are your friends, if I may ask my lady?" Terren said.

"Xirel and Loki."

The whispers started up again all around her, until Mother Weaver silenced them.

"If Kenshe comes for her, can we defeat him?" Terren asked.

Mother Weaver pulled a pouch from her belt and then reached in it to pull out several grey stones. She threw them on the ground before her, then kneeled and touched one after the other with her index finger. Two from the Pack helped back to her feet when she lacked the strength to stand up straight again. "The Atrum Lord has lost favour with the Caelestis from his countless atrocities. But our actions must coincide with this Fay's will as well. Tell me Ubi, would you stay with us?"

Ubi didn't know what she wanted to do at this point. All she knew is that she couldn't go back to Kenshe, and that her heart wouldn't let her face Nafury. She had broken her promise to him to be honest. She had been too much of a coward to tell him everything, and now he might be dead because of her. All she could do was stay out of the way of everyone so that no one else got hurt because of her.

Terren stood up and closed the distance between them.

Ubi looked around the Pack, and then for what had been bothering her since she arrived. The Pack's shifts were completely fearless of her. It was as if they had no fear of her harming their hosts... Because their hosts were already dead. "You're Awls?"

Terren smiled and nodded.

"Wait, but you called her 'Mother,'" Ubi pointed out, and looked at the old ayame. Her shift rested near the entrance to the cave.

"That's because I gave birth to each and every one of them, child," Mother Weaver explained. "I have served in three different Packs in my lifetime. While I am still alive, my children have taken different paths towards their Fates."

Ubi was stunned now, as there were at least two dozen of the phelan Awls, all males from what she could tell. She couldn't imagine losing so many children to death. "I'm sorry," she said solemnly.

"Why ever are you sorry, child? I sense that you cannot hear the Great Dragon yet. His voice is always on the wind. His will is a constant vibration beneath our feet and in the Animus Threads. When Sentry fall to Aster to become Awls, they only succeed if they accept that

Aragmoth is this world. My children were spared by the Great Dragon and given near-immortality. I do not mourn for them, for they are still very much with me."

"That and we are the one and only Ghost Pack," another phelan Awl said. "If Kenshe wants a fight, I hope he's ready to lose."

"Do not boast, Hiro," Mother Weaver scorned him. "Kenshe is the son of one of the Four Generals, one of the very first Awls. The blood of Solar in his veins will give him the fire to fight well past any normal phelan. He will be your greatest challenge yet."

"Of course, Mother," Hiro said apologetically. "But if we win, may we keep the prize?"

Ubi's face went red from how the phelan Awl was looking at her now.

"If she knows with Loki, then he will likely come looking for her soon," Terren said. Hiro sulked and walked away at that. "But it would be an honour to protect you until then. The dragon Awl is a powerful ally to make." He reached out his hand to her then. "If you want to stay with us, we can protect you."

Ubi calculated her options, then took his hand. She only wanted to see Loki and Xirel again, even if she had no right to.

Ubi had forgotten what it was like to be surrounded by so many friendly people. The Weaver's Pack had loosened up around her, and now they were all laughing about random things from Earth around the fire.

"I want to drive one of those car things one day," Hiro said, as he looked at Ubi. "If I ever go to Earth, it's the first thing I'm going for. Have you ever driven one?"

"No, you have to be a certain age to get a license for it. And you have to have money to afford a car. I've been moved around in them, though," Ubi replied.

"How fast do they go? Are they faster than us?" Hiro asked.

"Not a chance," Terren said, certain.

Ubi laughed as the others did the same. Then their laughter was suddenly interrupted by a low hum of a Call, and they looked to Mother Weaver.

"Kenshe's here. Let's give him our best show," Terren said, and took on the form of his phelan spirit.

The others of the Pack did the same, and Ubi was left alone with the old ayame. "Will they be okay?"

'The Great Dragon favours us today, do not worry yourself. My children, as they are now, have never been defeated in battle.'

Ubi got up and fixed Mother Weaver's blanket on her shoulders. Then she stood up straight and looked in the direction that she could hear Kenshe calling for her. A thick, white mist filled the air. It blinded the sight of anyone who looked for something past the distance of their own feet. She thought that if the Great Dragon did serve any kind of justice, this might be it. Maybe today Kenshe would pay for the lives he took at Xirel's home.

She sat next to Mother Weaver and closed her eyes. She searched for Terren's psi and found it. He returned comforting thoughts to her, before his psi focused back on the battle at hand.

Kenshe knew he was in for a fight when the mist began to rise around him. The Ghost Pack had been a myth; a ghost story to scare the youngsters with, only it seemed very real now. The entire area of Threads had been weaved against him, and any one that he touched could spring an attack on him. "Ubi!" he called out, knowing that he had to get her to reach out to him if he was going to get anywhere. "Ubi, look, I'm sorry. I didn't mean what I said. And you know I hate Nafury and Xirel, so what business would I have telling them anything?"

"GO AWAY!" she yelled back.

Kenshe pinpointed the direction of her voice. But before he could make a move, a Thread to his legs snapped, and it sent him tumbling forward to the ground. He kept his calm as the teeth from the phelan Awl came down on him next. It passed through him, as it was still bound to the Laws of Aragmoth. At least there was someone on his side. As long as he didn't make himself a threat, he wouldn't be eaten. Only that wouldn't stop the Awls from snapping every life Thread in him. The black phelan vanished back into the mist like a shadow, and Kenshe slowly got back to his feet.

"You heard the lady," a voice said from a different direction in the mist. "She does not want to go with you anywhere."

"I don't recall asking you for your permission. Now get out of my way!" Kenshe shouted back.

"Not going to happen," another voice replied.

Kenshe felt another Thread snap in him, and he wiped his nose as blood started to drip from it. "You have some nerve to attack me! I am the Atrum Lord and protected by the Caelestis!"

"The Goddess has forsaken you as you have long forgotten her," the first voice said. Kenshe's legs were made numb, and he was forced to the ground again. His hands caught him and he stayed still, trying to calculate which Thread they would go for next.

"Her daughter has been given to us," the second voice said.

"I don't think so," Kenshe spat back and caught the Threads to the voice as they appeared for a split second. He cut them with his nails, before realizing his stupid mistake.

The red-haired Awl unshifted and rushed at him, delivering a kick to his face that threw him backwards.

"I think he is trying to *kill* us, brother," his attacker mocked. Moments later, the mist engulfed the phelan Awl again.

"Somehow he has survived this long despite being intolerably stupid," the first voice said. "You cannot kill what is already dead you fool. Leave before we kill you for wasting our time."

Another foot hit Kenshe in the back, and he buckled over as blood gushed from his mouth to the ground. He couldn't take much more of this. A rush of estus energy surged past Kenshe then. The hatred and sadness of it threatened to drag him into the ground and to his grave. "Ubi I would never hurt you! Sybl and Kas were everything to me! Please stop this!"

"Yet you were weak and did not protect them," another phelan said.

The Threads were lifted under Kenshe, and he was thrown into the air. He fell a meter before colliding with the ground on his back. Kenshe could feel his life draining from him fast now as he hurt too much to roll over. There were just too many of the Awl phelan to defend himself against.

"That is not true," a female voice spoke.

Kenshe looked to the side as the mist lifted all at once, and dispersed into clear air. He could see all twenty-four of the Pack he was up against now. Cursing himself for being such an idiot to tackle such odds alone, he lay flat on his back. He heard footsteps, and looked up to the only face he wanted to see. Sybl's glowing blue eyes looked back down at him. "I'm sorry. Sybl... Please...forgive me."

"You're an idiot, Kenshe!" the voice spat back, but it was different now. The image of Sybl that he had imagined vanished and left Prisca looking down at him. Her red eyes were furious. "What in the seven Hells do you think you're doing?"

"Dying," was all Kenshe could reply and closed his eyes.

"Sister, what are you doing here?" Terren asked, walking closer to them.

"What does it look like?" Prisca replied with a bitter tone. "Mother," she called, and the old woman began to slowly make her way over with Ubi. "What is going on here?"

"Kenshe wishes to take the Fay against her will. I was not going to let that happen."

"By killing him? Are you insane, old woman? If the Caelestis can see us now, she would never forgive you! Kenshe was given to her and he answers only to Sybl!"

"Do not attempt to tell me what to do!" Mother Weaver snapped back. "We are not of your corrupted Order!"

"That Fay," Prisca said, looking at Ubi, "is the Atrum's responsibility. It was her father who ruled over it before Kenshe. She is coming with us." Prisca kneeled down then, and started to heal Kenshe's wounds.

"She can't see yet...what we know," Kenshe said

through painful breaths as Prisca patched his inner wounds back together with her limited aeri.

Prisca understood what he was talking about, and walked over to Ubi.

Ubi stepped back to avoid being grabbed, but Prisca was faster and caught her tunic. Then the Caller pressed her hand against her forehead. Ubi tried to struggle free, then realized that she wasn't standing in the same place anymore. Ubi looked at Prisca before her, then looked to where she did, as the ayame's memory melded into her own. She saw her father.

The gardens at the back of the Sanctus were vibrant and beautiful. If you stood back and looked at the rows of flowers, you could see a line separating them. The side of light were alive and healthy, while those in darkness were dreary. The line between consisted of roses like what could be found on Earth.

Kas walked the line for a few moments, before setting down a small pail of blue paint. Eyes watched him from all sides, and it didn't seem to bother him.

Three ayame had taken up playfully laughing at him when he picked up the paintbrush. They seemed desperate to get his attention. The laughter stopped a few minutes later, and Kas looked for what could have sent the ayame away so suddenly. It was Sybl.

"Are you painting flowers?" she asked as she walked over.

"Just the roses," he corrected. He glanced only momentarily at her and away from his chosen rose bush.

"Phelan can't see red, can they?"

"We can see it enough to know that it is connected to something important." He snapped the one free that he had finished painting blue, and offered it to her.

"But all your eyes are red—how do you see the eyes of other phelan?" She took the rose from him.

"We see each other's intentions instead of red, as the eyes are a reflection of the soul."

"Like blood." Sybl smelled the rose. But it wasn't doing much for her. "Am I like the only creature on this whole planet who has blue eyes?"

"You are one of the few who have the colour of pure destiny in their eyes. You should be more than content with that."

"You mean there's someone else other than me?"

Kas didn't answer and started painting another rose. He dipped his fingers in the blue paint, and touched her nose before she could dodge it.

"Hey!" Sybl tried to wipe the paint off of her nose, only to smear it worse in the process.

"Perhaps I should try more unconventional methods to help you remember your past life."

"You're so mean," Sybl said, as she took the spare brush from the pail. "Just for that, I'm painting your entire room a bright red while you sleep."

"I have nothing to fear then, as I have not slept since I was a newborn."

Sybl looked at the rose bush for where to start practicing.

"Which one is the most red to you?"

"Um... They're all like the same color of red," Sybl replied.

"Then your best guess."

Sybl started to paint a rose, before realizing that it was trickier than it looked. When she couldn't get it as neat as Kas could, she decided to paint him while he looked the other way.

He wiped the blue off of his face and onto his white sleeve. "Try that again."

"Okay." She laughed and went for him again, but he caught her and tackled her to the ground. Then he used her own brush to paint more of her face.

"Hey! Stop!" Sybl tried to get free of him, but he didn't let her go until she was mostly blue, and they couldn't laugh anymore.

Kas released her and stood up. He smiled as he realized that in painting her, he had painted most of himself as well.

"I'm so not feeling the color of 'pure destiny' right now," Sybl said as she sat up. She tried to get her long wavy strands of hair back in order, including her newest blue ones. Then she stopped running her fingers through her hair and stared up at him.

They stared at each for a long while, each of them deciphering the other's thoughts.

Kas sat back down, and looked at his rose bush. "There are not enough flowers here to cure the world's sufferings. The Aeger cannot be cured with flower petals, and few spirits are healed by their beauty."

"One Fay cannot save the world. But it's important that we show that we haven't given up and keep trying," Sybl said.

Kas nodded in agreement. "Perhaps the stubborn ones against us simply need to be painted a different color. Tomorrow, I will try purple."

Sybl picked up the blue rose he had given her. "Nah, try white."

"The red will bleed through..."

Sybl giggled as she got to her feet.

Kas looked back at the rose bush with a more determined expression. "Keep trying, I get it."

The memory faded, and Ubi blinked as her eyes returned to the present. "You were one of the ayame watching him?"

"I was still very young back then," Prisca explained. "The Atrum may not be the perfect sanctuary like the Sanctus was, but it is all we have now. Your father was its rightful ruler, as was your mother. You've been fighting the wrong side, Ubi. Kenshe, the Order—all of it has not forgotten your mother or Kas."

Ubi stepped back for a moment as she tried to take it all in. She looked at Terren. He sat patiently in his phelan form, waiting for her to speak of what she would do next. "How can I trust you? Especially after the massacre Kenshe made at the Efereal Mountains?"

"The Awls are dangerous," Kenshe said, sitting up with a groan. "You know why and you've seen it for yourself. Your very blood is what our enemy is using to control them. If you stay here, then the same thing will happen to this Pack what happened just now at the Efereal Mountains. The one who is after you isn't going to stop."

Ubi looked at Terren, as the last thing she wanted to do was put them in danger.

"It's alright," Terren replied. "Kenshe has a point. There has been unusual stress on the Threads that connect my kind to each other. Whether your blood's power is responsible or not, we would not want to put you in harms way if we should turn. You will be safer in my sister's care."

Ubi looked at Prisca as she helped Kenshe to his feet.

"We will not be far if you change your mind," Mother Weaver said and touched her shoulder. "You may call on our help whenever you need."

"Thank you," Ubi said, and then turned and walked over to Kenshe. They both stared at one another for a while, before he stepped back and shifted into his phelan form. Crouching down, Ubi climbed onto his back and he started to leave right after.

"Sister," Terren said, looking at Prisca.

"I know, Terren," Prisca replied. "I will take care of her. With this thing taking control of the Awls, we will be closer to stopping it with the Fay's help. If anything, she will draw her mother's spirit closer and the Caelestis will protect us."

"Stay close to Aragmoth, daughter," Mother Weaver said. Then the old ayame turned and started to walk back to camp. "The caels are not here, they are with Him still."

"You too, Mother," Prisca replied, then shifted into her cat-like phelan form and followed after Kenshe.

TWENTY

Ubi felt like screaming when Kenshe pulled the dress over her head by force.

"You make this a lot harder than it has to be," he said, straightening the black and blue garment on her. Then he started to tie the laces on her back. "I won't have you moving around my castle smelling like death and looking like I dragged you out of a gutter."

"Your ayame are even worse than you!" Ubi spat back. "Stop touching me!"

"Of all things they think that I might fall for you," Kenshe sneered in her ear.

"That's a laugh. You are the worst individual I've have ever met. I would rather die a thousand times more!"

"Likewise," Kenshe said. He tightened the last of her dress to an uncomfortable tightness. "To think I was so damn close to being free of you."

"Lord Kenshe," Prisca said, appearing in the doorway.

"Oh thank Aragmoth," Kenshe said and pushed Ubi forward and away from him. "I need you to watch this brat until one of her caretakers come for her. I can't take her shit anymore."

"Of course," Prisca said and looked at Ubi with her unreadable red eyes.

"Please don't leave a mark on her. You are the only ayame I can trust with this. Keeping her in one piece is currently very important to me."

"I won't let you down, my lord. Please leave her to me."

Kenshe nodded and left the room at that.

They stared at one another for some moments, before Ubi gave up and went to sit on the bed given to her.

"I must say, it's amusing to see Sybl's character in someone who looks so much like Kas. Surely Fate was being cruel by not dealing your cards in the opposite," Prisca started.

"I don't think so. My father was an animal."

Prisca's eyes widened in disbelief of Ubi's words. Then she began to pick up Ubi's old, torn clothes and tidy up the room. "Your father was anything but an animal. He was magnificent. He was perfect in every sense. When he took control over the Atrum after Vanir's death, the phelan rejoiced. Equally, the Suzerain Continent wept when he was lost. He was a leader and a soldier, but most importantly, his very aura shone of the Fay he was."

"And my mother?" Ubi asked, changing the topic to one she was interested in.

"I was still small when I met her for the first time as you have seen. My first impression of her was that she was some filthy human beggar. When I later learned that she was a Fay, I wouldn't believe it for a long while. Your mother was hard to understand, but I don't think it was because she was a human."

"Oh?" Ubi asked, cautious to where Prisca would take this conversation.

Prisca put the dirty clothes she had in hand in a basket near the door. Another ayame came by within moments to pick it up and take it away. She brushed her black hair back over her shoulder and straightened her grey dress. Prisca then wandered around the room, trying to find the right words. "You would have had to hear her Nova to understand her, I think. When she sang, half the world's Threads shuddered and reacted to her will. While she looked harmless, if not useless on the outside, I think that was just a face she wore to hide her true power. She was truly a raw power that wasn't supposed to be here, let alone exist."

"What do you mean?"

"According to the Texts," Prisca said as she went to sit next to Ubi, "there should always be a Fay of darkness and one of light. That is how balance between life and death is maintained. But Sybl was a balance of both on her own. She was like the great Asteria of the first Aster. A Sylph, capable of wielding light and darkness at will. Maybe Asteria gave her that power before her destruction. No one really knows."

"If she's so strong, why doesn't she come back from the dead to help us?" Ubi asked.

"Oh, I'll bet that she will," Prisca replied. "This unseen enemy will see its last once it reveals itself, I'll bet my tail on it." She stood up and headed to the door then. "Now, will you come down for dinner, or should I have it brought up here?"

"I'll stay here, thanks," Ubi replied. "Please make sure it's vegetarian as well."

"Vege—what?" Prisca asked.

"No meat, please."

One of Prisca's eye's twitched and she continued to leave. "Of course. Our chef has been in need of a challenge as of late..."

"Prisca, wait," Ubi called after the ayame.

Prisca returned to the room, faking patience for the Fay. "What is it?"

"What was my mother to Kenshe? I want to know why he flipped out on me like he did in the Keol over her."

"She was like a mother to him. She was the only mother he ever had."

"What, seriously? Where is his?" Ubi asked in

disbelief.

"The daoran is still alive to my knowledge. She didn't accept him since he was born like a True, and his father brought him to the Sanctus. For a long time I thought that Kenshe felt something more for Sybl. But I have studied him closely all these years. I'm certain that it was nothing more than a child's affection he had for her. When Sybl died, he was no longer that child."

Ubi nodded in understanding, and Prisca left and closed the door behind her. She got to her feet and looked around the room. On the dresser, she found a sword on a stand. She picked it up, curious to who it belonged to. But she didn't know how to read its Thread. She brought it over to the bed and sat down with it on her lap, and closed her eyes. Touching the fairy pendant on her neck, then the hilt of the blade, she tried to use it to see into the weapon. A familiar voice pulled her into it.

Kenshe wandered lost for a while, between the living and the realm of death. When he didn't find Ubi as fast as he wanted to, he decided to resort to his phelan senses to try and pick up on her. He knew that venturing so deep into Aragmoth would require a great deal of luck to get back out again. The lost Fay was untrained on how to do all this, and if he didn't find her soon, she would likely be lost in limbo forever. There was a potentially lethal difference between Dreaming and Dreamwalking. With Dreamwalking, your soul left your body with little more than a Thread or two to lead you back.

He caught her scent and jogged through the fog towards it. He found her, sitting quietly before a pond of gas and water. He concluded that this was a part of Aragmoth's mind that had been made to resemble the first Aster. Such climate and environment had only ever existed on the first. "Ubi." She turned to look at him without any kind of emotion on her face.

"It's so warm here," she said, as her fingers made ripples in the water.

Despite his better judgement, Kenshe felt himself feeling sorry for her again. "What are you doing here? I found you with your father's sword—are you looking for him?"

"Is that who it belonged to?" Ubi asked.

"We should go," Kenshe said and crouched down beside her. "This place isn't safe."

"Why should I go back?"

"Don't talk like that. You're needed alive," Kenshe insisted.

"Am I?"

"Well, you can die later if you want, but I won't have

Nafury killing me for leaving you here." He picked her up into his arms, and was thankful when she didn't struggle. When he stood up straight again, the scenery around them had been changed to resemble the Keol.

He turned to look in all directions, before his eyes saw a young man staring back at him, almost out of range of his sight. He squinted to look closer, and saw that it was Kas. "If you wanted to say anything to your father before we left, now is the time."

Ubi turned her face to look where he did, and stared at the figure for a while. "I don't want to see him."

"Suit yourself," Kenshe said and started to follow their lifelines back to consciousness. He had only taken a few steps when the ground shook. Out of nowhere, Kas appeared in front of him. "Master Kas?"

"Kenshe," Kas replied. "Put her down and go."

"What? Why?"

"She will only bring destruction if she returns to Aster. I have foreseen it," Kas replied.

"Maybe you have, but that hasn't happened yet." Kenshe tried to walk around Kas, but now the dark Fay's outstretched sword blocked his path. "Ubi is coming back to the living, with me, right now."

The grip on Kas' sword loosened. "Have you seen her?"

"Have you not?" Kenshe asked in concern. He knew that Kas could only be talking about Sybl. "Shouldn't she be here with you?"

"She will not speak with me," Kas said, and looked at Ubi. "I miss her more than I can bear."

Ubi looked away from him and hid her face in Kenshe's black shirt.

"I need you to forgive me, Ubi. I would wait an eternity if I could, but Aster does not have that long. Your mother cannot hold Aragmoth together by herself much longer. I need to be at her side, and for that I need you to forgive me for what I did to you."

Kenshe looked around briefly as he pondered a problem he had not thought he might encounter till now. Kas could have him wandering in this limbo for as long as their bodies were alive if he wanted to.

Ubi didn't answer.

Kas reached out a careful hand and touched her forehead. She shook his frozen touch off, agitated. Moments after she did, he vanished in a swirl of shadow. Then the scenery changed again.

Kenshe looked around and found that he had been instantly brought back to Kas' room that he had given to Ubi. He sat up and looked at her as she began to wake up. He took the sword from her hands and removed his own. Setting Kas' blade in his sheathe, he put his own on the stand. He wasn't in the mood for anymore visits to the realm of death.

"Kenshe?" Ubi asked as she rubbed her eyes.

"Don't do anything stupid like that again," he said angrily and started to leave the room. "Your food is cold now, and you can eat it like that."

Ubi sat up and looked at her nightstand where a tray with water and a plate of salad sat. It was a cold-served dish to begin with. She looked at the dresser and the sword there. She could tell right away that Kenshe had taken away her father's blade. She left the room and ran down the hall after him. "Give me back my father's blade!"

Everyone around them stopped in their tracks as Kenshe turned to face the Fay. He replied with a flat-out, "No."

Ubi knew her power over his shift wouldn't work, neither would a fist fight. She looked around, forcing her will on the other shifters in the hall. They responded and turned their teeth on Kenshe, to the shock of their hosts.

"Go ahead, brat. I need to spread your blood around to the Packs, anyways. There is no one in this hallway who can kill me."

One of the guard's spirits went for Kenshe. In one swift movement he had Kas' blade in hand and slashed it across the phelan's face. It reeled back in pain, and put the others into a hesitate state.

"You have no control over your power except by reflex. If you want your father's blade back that badly, I will see you in the throne room in the morning. If you prove to me that you're someone other than an idiot, you can have it back," Kenshe said.

Ubi's rage boiled over, as she could do little more than watch him turn and leave for downstairs. "I should have let them kill you!"

"Try harder next time," he shouted back. "Because at the rate you're going I'm guaranteed to die as an old phelan!"

TWENTY-ONE

Nafury was left with more time than he wanted to feel sorry for himself. The encounter with the Sentry at the Efereal Mountains had not ended well. The Sentry had proved to be the lesser of their problems as well. Xirel had succumbed to their mind control and Nafury had no choice but to kill him. Loki and himself would have been killed had he hesitated another moment.

He had flown non-stop to the Torian Continent afterwards, and he wasn't sure why. He had only managed to fly as far as the Casus Beli Canyon before his strength gave out. Nafury hadn't seen everything that had happened as Alexia took over much of the last hours. But he could still feel his claws crushing the life out of Xirel. It was all he saw now, even as his own wounds continued to bleed out onto the pink flowers around him. Nafury remained vaguely aware of something watching him from a short distance away. He wondered if he would die today, perhaps by what stalked him. The presence crept silently closer, until two orange eyes from the face of a dragon hovered over his face. "Loki."

"What are you doing here? Ubi is the other way."

Nafury looked at the sky behind the dragon. "Why are you here?"

"I've just come to smell the flowers and visit my castle," Loki lied.

Nafury didn't have the strength left in him to endure Loki's carefree attitude. "I can't go back there and face her after what I did. "

"Xirel knew that his time was coming to an end. We can sometimes see the future too, you know? She will understand if you explain what happened," Loki insisted.

"No, she won't. This has ruined all chance of gaining forgiveness from her."

"You're just depressed and not thinking straight. Did you want me to heal those for you?" the dragon asked, looking at the wound in his shoulder.

"I'm fine."

"It's not all about you, you know? Just what would be said of me if I left you to bleed to death here?" The dragon's face retreated for a moment, and Nafury looked to his side as a green mist drifted past him. The human-like appearance of Loki stood up straight, and light green hair fell over his shoulders. The Awl's youthful eyes returned his stare. Loki had been born before him, but since he was an Awl now, he hadn't aged a day since.

The Awl didn't ask this time for permission as he sat on his knees and put a hand on Nafury's shoulder. Loki used his aeri to pull the wound together, and then did the same to Nafury's leg. Afterward, he quickly looked him over for the last wound he sensed.

"That one doesn't heal so easily," Nafury said, guessing what Loki was looking for.

"You're not the only one with a broken heart." Loki remained determined, and set a steady hand over Nafury's chest. "We can fix that one too. But not if you give up here."

Nafury didn't pay the Awl's attempt to heal the un-healable much mind. That was until he took notice that his heartbeat had evened out. He glanced at Loki and the Awl returned a small smile.

"That will work for now."

Nafury sat up with difficultly. He guessed that he had lost more blood than he thought. As the blood drained from his head, a flashback of his claws tearing into Xirel flashed past his mind again. It was almost powerful enough to drop him back to the grass as he pressed the sides of his head.

"You should stay still for a while. You're only human."

"Thanks for reminding me," Nafury replied.

Loki brought his knees up and was content to use his

stare to keep him company.

"Why are you looking at me like that?" Nafury asked.

"I feel like I'm looking at a ghost when I look at you. You don't even realize yourself how much you look like her."

"I wish I could see her again, especially now," Nafury replied. He feared that Loki might try to kill him yet if he spoke anymore of Sybl.

"Well, today is your lucky day cause she's standing right there." Loki looked to the other side of Nafury and across the field.

Nafury moved so fast this time, his head felt like it would spin off of him. When he could see straight again, he looked everywhere for Sybl, but only saw Sial. The kyrie remained his ever-faithful follower. "That wasn't funny, Loki. My sister is dead," Nafury replied with a bitter tone.

"I was being serious. Look again," Loki said.

Nafury sighed but did as told, and took notice that Sial's eyes had changed color. The kyrie's were no longer purple, but the same sapphire blue as his own. "Sybl?"

She didn't reply as she walked closer to him.

"She's hurt too, you know?" Loki said, then looked at the kyrie. "Sybl, we need your guidance more than ever."

Sial turned his face to the side for a moment before looking back at them. "I was wrong."

Nafury was on his feet now when her voice came out

of the kyrie. "Sister? Are you really in there?"

"I thought that we could go to Earth and uncover who is behind this madness, but I was wrong. We can't go there, and we can't stay here and wait to die."

"Do you know who is doing this?" Loki asked, getting to his feet.

"Before Xirel died, I tried to grab his Threads and keep him alive and here. But I couldn't hold onto him. Not because I didn't have the strength, but because of who was holding the other end of his Threads."

Nafury had his hands on Sial now, trying to find a way to pull her from the creature. "Who was it? Who are we fighting?"

"I'm sorry, Nafury. I didn't know. When he vanished from the realm of death, I knew he had gone to Earth. I didn't know anything of what he was thinking of doing there," Sybl said.

Nafury took a moment to put her words together. "Cirrus? You can't be serious—why would he do this?"

"It's my fault. The last thing he said to me was that he would find a way to free me. He thinks that by being what I am, and within Aragmoth, that I'm the Great Dragon's prisoner."

Loki brought his hand to the back of his neck as he tried to compile everything as well. "I had so many chances to kill that bastard, and now this..."

"You can't let him succeed," Sybl insisted. "If he

disconnects me now from Aragmoth, Aster will cease to exist. All of us will return to being spirit slaves on Earth or fall into oblivion. The Great Dragon's reserve strength is long spent."

Nafury pulled his hair back and paced a few steps, before turning back to her. "Can he actually do it?"

"Nafury, listen to me. Aster comes first. You must stay here."

"Sybl, if there is a way to bring you back to the living, nothing is going to get in my way of that," Nafury said with a serious tone.

"This is beyond just you and me. Thousands of lives have to be protected. Promise me you won't go to him," Sybl pleaded.

"I can't do that," Nafury said and took a step back. "You and Cirrus are everything to me."

Sial seemed to lose his balance for a moment, before he lifted his head high again. His eyes had returned to being purple, and Sybl's presence was gone.

"No, wait!" he called to her, but it was no use. Nafury fell back to the grass at a sit, as it felt like she had cut a piece of his heart out all over again.

"The Caelestis has made her wishes known," Loki said.

"I am going to save her," Nafury replied, and looked at Loki. "Cirrus forced me to kill Xirel, so he's trying to make her appear so he can trap her. If I can save Aster as well, fine."

The Awl shifted back into his dragon form and sat down, before looking in the direction of the Falls. His long, green tail twitched back and forth in contemplation. "I owe Sybl everything I am, but we must obey her. She would not put us in harms way or methods of doing what's needed."

"You're thinking about something. What is it?" Nafury said, as he tuned into Loki's Threads.

"The Falls might know more about what's going on with Earth than we do. Their Tech has been watching it for some time. Maybe we can find a way to save Sybl and stop Cirrus without having to face off with him. But the griffin shifter who lives there is violent and mad."

"He was Kenshe's friend," Nafury said out of memory. A memory flashed past his eyes of the look Gwa had given him when he had returned from Earth. Right after Sybl had died. It was that of pure contempt. He shifted into his dragon form in a rush of white mist. "So we'll force Kenshe to get us near him. Let's try your idea," he said and looked at him. "If it doesn't work, then I will do this my way."

Loki nodded in agreement, and sprung into the air as Nafury followed.

TWENTY-TWO

Kenshe would be lying if he said that he wasn't getting a certain kick out of tormenting Ubi. She made it too easy. Her rage made her efforts to hold onto his lifelines next to impossible. With her ability to control his shift disabled, he felt like he was kicking a toddler around. He pulled the Threads to her legs, and she was flipped backwards onto her backside. Revenge was fun too. Inside he laughed as she squeaked and rubbed her sore tailbone. "I thought you wanted to kill me and take back your father's sword? I'm still waiting..."

"You go from being purrfully cute to a complete asshole often?" Ubi asked.

"You can still purr?" another phelan asked from where he sat lounging near the window.

"Shut it, Feryl," Kenshe snapped back.

Ubi used his distracted state to attack the Threads to

his heart, and let out a cheer as Kenshe's eyes winced in pain.

"Nice try, but I'm not in the mood for heartburn," Kenshe replied. He retaliated by pulling Ubi's arms up and over her head, before pulling the Threads to her stomach. She keeled over, as if hit there with a punch.

Feryl was busy waiting for Prisca who sat across from him to finish eating. Their rest wouldn't last long. The Efereal Mountains was likely the Sentries' first stop on the Suzerain Continent. The Atrum would be attacked next. Every available Caller was keeping the Calls through the Threads active. They were their only early warning defence. Their sad, low-pitched song would skip a beat if the wrong creature touched the Animus Thread. It would also pinpoint where their invisible enemy was.

Meanwhile, the males were cleaning, cooking, washing and serving. Feryl didn't mind the switch of duties much, as the downtime gave him the chance to fix and play with his Tech screen. There wasn't much technology left at the Atrum now. With the Falls and griffins' downfall, most Tech had become useless relics without their expertise. He looked at Prisca as her eyes gazed out the window, focused on something she heard, again. He picked up the fork and gently touched her chin, where she absent-mindedly took bite. For the other phelan, it gave them the rare opportunity to mingle with the ayame. On any other day, they were untouchable. He remembered that when Vanir had reigned over the Atrum, it was much the same. "You're just like your father," Feryl said, looking at Kenshe. "All tough and cold only on the outside."

Kenshe ignored the phelan shifter and kept his focus on Ubi. "It's a miracle you survived this long." He picked up a glass of water from a nearby table and took a few sips while she struggled to recover from his attack.

"You are being rather harsh on her," Prisca said. The Caller only momentarily pulled her attention back into the room.

"She has a lot of rage that needs to be diffused. Should I give her a wooden stick to hit with so she can learn to be a carpenter, instead?" Kenshe asked.

"Her mother was a wonderful artist," Prisca replied. "Kas knew how to incorporate that strength of Sybl's into her training and it was effective."

Kenshe hadn't thought of that. All he knew of Ubi's interests at the moment was that she wanted to kill him.

Feryl and Tank both found the topic interesting and looked at Ubi.

"What?" she asked, having found her lost wind. "Why are you staring at me?"

"What are you good at, Ubi?" Feryl asked.

Ubi blinked a few times as she thought on it. She looked at the screen-thin computer in Feryl's hand.

Focusing her energy on it, she made it come on and the drive run again.

That was an attention stopper, as Feryl put the Tech carefully down on the table. It hadn't come on for the phelan shifter until now. "Holy shit. She's got a griffin shifter's electricity or something in her..."

Kenshe walked over to the table and looked at the screen. "Gwa would like you," he thought aloud.

"Is that crazy bat still alive?" Feryl asked. He gently tapped the images on the screen as to not break what had been fixed for him.

Suddenly the sound of the Call changed to include the True's howls. Everyone froze in place while Kenshe quickly deciphered it. "The Council is here. Let's go." He started out of the room and his Pack followed.

Ubi found herself alone in the throne room after everyone left. She looked around before going over to Kenshe's dark- wood chair. The feeling of superiority came over her as she sat down and crossed one leg over the other. Ubi imagined her mother sitting in the same spot. She wondered what Sybl would have done if she were here. Closing her eyes, she willed her necklace to answer her question. She reopened them, and found her father standing before her. At first she panicked, before it became clear that she was now sharing her seat in this particular memory.

Kas stepped up beside a dark-skinned phelan shifter. "You ceased being my father the day you killed my mother."

"Of course," Vanir said as he shifted in the dark wood of the intricately carved chair. His straight, black hair draped over it like a cloak. "You are here to talk about peace. That being the case, I would like to offer you your rightful title of Prince."

The guard looked at Kas, with a glance that suggested he was worried he might actually consider it.

"Why now? Why after denying that I am of your blood for so long?" Kas asked.

"One of my Callers had a Vision of the Asterian Caelestis' return. If it is accurate, as most of hers are, it will be soon. Hence why I believe that settling the dispute between the Sanctus and the Atrum would serve both our interests."

"Is that concern in your voice I hear? After all these years has your conscience finally surfaced from its withering darkness to see that my mother was right?"

"Your mother was the finest of my Callers, until she lost her way. It seems only Kira's Visions have proven to withstand Time and stay their course," Vanir said.

"If the Sanctus is nothing but a symbol for the lost to you, then perhaps you are happiest lost and in waiting. You forget that I too can foresee the future, only I never needed you or anyone else to tell me what I already knew was right. When the Caelestis returns, I will not share her for a title, or for your Empire, or with you. All the bribes you have will not bring me any closer to your corruption any more than it will her."

"One of your former Custos has seen the potential in allying with me and brings her back as we speak," Vanir replied.

"I pity the fools you sent for her then, because they will not live long."

"If the caels are returning to Aster, then the true fools are those who sit and do nothing while waiting for redemption." Vanir leaned forward and rested his hands and arms on his legs. "They will bring us only death."

"The dead can still hear prayers. I know death will not touch myself or those who seek shelter in the Sanctus. So enjoy your reign of fear while it lasts for it will not be for much longer. I am High Priest of the Sanctus, son of Kira and leader of the Custos. Your words are of the same nothing to me that they were to my mother," Kas finished bitterly.

Ubi opened her eyes to the present after her father turned to leave. For a brief moment, she wondered if her circumstances would be different if her father were alive. She heard a shuffle, and looked up through the tears that had snuck into her eyes. Kenshe was standing at the door, impatiently waiting for her.

"Are you comfortable?" he asked.

"That phelan shifter said that Fay bring only death. He must have been talking about me," Ubi replied, as she remembered Vanir's words.

Kenshe took a moment to tune into her psi to see who she was talking about. "Maybe Vanir was. Do you still want to kill everyone and everything?"

"I've narrowed it down to just you," Ubi replied in a ice-cold tone.

"Well, jeeze. Here I was being nice by coming all the way back up here to let you know that you uncle is unfortunately still alive. And he's here."

"Is Xirel with him?" Ubi asked and jumped up from the chair.

"Didn't see him, don't care. I have my own problems in the War Room downstairs. Keep it down for the next few hours lest you scare away my army."

Ubi pushed past him and ran for the stairs.

There was a long hesitation in the War Room of the Atrum as no one wanted to speak first. Nafury's unexpected intrusion had changed the topic from Sentry to him. Many of the phelan Pack leaders were old enough to remember the sheer power that the White Death had. And the devastation and death that Daath had inflicted on their lives.

Nafury turned around and watched as Kenshe came into the room. He could sense Ubi just outside the doors.

She was likely intimidated from entering by how tense the air was in here.

"Is there something we can help you with, Fallen Prince?" Kenshe asked as he took his seat at the head of the table.

"I need you to come with me to the Falls," Nafury replied, getting straight to the point.

"Why?"

Nafury glanced around the room, before looking back at Kenshe. "Because I spoke with her."

Kenshe shook his head, pretending at first to not know who he was talking about. "You spoke with the Caelestis?"

"Yes."

The room became loud with whispers.

"And she told you to go to the Falls?"

"No. My sister," Nafury said with emphasis, "is struggling to keep the latest threat to Aster at bay. The Sentry are not going to stop coming, and they're after her."

"Let's say I believe you for a minute, what use are the Falls? It's nothing but ruins and griffin bones now," Kenshe replied.

"Because we share the same enemy, and I need alternatives in defeating him. Particularly as he has a means to restore Sybl to life."

The room began to talk amongst themselves again. Everyone was curious to know who they were up against.

"Sybl is the only one keeping Aragmoth alive after the extent of damage you caused to Aster," Kenshe stated flatly. "She can't return to the living, or this world will die."

"Then we are right back to square one with each other," Nafury replied. "Because if there is a way to bring her back to life, I have every intention of doing just that."

"You would see Aster perish to restore your sister to life?" Kenshe asked. "What does she have to say about that?"

Nafury looked to the side and didn't answer.

Loki came into the room and briefly looked the Council members over. He set his eyes on Kenshe. "The Falls has been watching Earth for a while. We're looking for a way to save both Aster and Sybl."

"Why am I talking to you, traitor?" Kenshe asked. "Where's Xirel?"

"He's dead," Nafury answered for Loki. "I killed him."

The room turned into an uproar now of panic.

"While you were a berserker no doubt?" a phelan shouted at him.

"He was being controlled by our enemy. Nafury had no choice. The mind control power our enemy has over the Awls is real," Loki said in Nafury's defence.

"Then how are you here?" another phelan asked.

"That is the starry-eyed one who communes with the Caelestis," an ayame's voice spoke. "Crystal and Estar's son."

"Sybl can't counter our enemy's power anymore. We have to act now," Loki insisted. "I could very easily be next—or any other Awl for that matter."

"This is bullshit," Kenshe suddenly burst out, turning all eyes on him. "There is no way in hell that Sybl would have allowed that to happen to Xirel. You've brought your lies into the wrong room, Nafury!"

"Have I? Didn't you try to kill him yourself just recently?" Nafury rebuked.

Kenshe pushed the chair out from under him and his fists hit the table. "The chimera Awls became our enemy when they left the Order! I did what was necessary!"

There was an eerie silence that filled the room now. Much of the Council had heard the rumours of the direct assault on the Awls and chimera. Those rumours were now facts. Only the sobs from Ubi just outside the door could be heard through the silence.

"You never attacked Xirel to protect the Atrum—you need to work on your lying," Loki said. He let go of Kenshe's infuriated, exposed Threads at that. "You did it to provoke her to respond to you. Only Sybl's always listening. You can bet all your souls that she never stopped listening to the ones who obey her will."

Kenshe finally calmed down enough to hear the crying from Ubi and sat back down. "You still have yet to tell us who the leader of our enemy is?"

"We're fighting Cirrus," Nafury replied, and the voices in the room returned to chaos.

"Quiet!" Kenshe shouted, as he was at his breaking point. "Cirrus is dead. He died after you killed Sybl!" His cold red eyes caught Nafury's with his words.

"Cirrus is the son of an Awl, and as such an Awl himself. He does not perish like we do," Loki replied. "If he is just a little as powerful as Alexia, then it is very likely that he has been pulling the strings. He also knows all of our weaknesses."

"So will you come with me to the Falls, or not?" Nafury asked, losing his patience with the Atrum Lord.

Kenshe was rubbing his forehead now as yet another impossible problem was dropped on him. He could tear the throat from any enemy, but he didn't know if he had it in him to go against Cirrus. "We'll leave in the hour. Go and get your niece away from my door before her tears stain what's left of the sanity in this room."

Nafury left to do just that, and closed the War Room's doors behind him. He found Ubi hugging her knees and rocking against the wall. "Ubi."

"You said... You said we would always be honest with each other," she said between stifled tears. "I should have told you everything—now Xirel is dead!"

He fell to his knees in front of her. He tried to touch her leg, but she slapped him away. Then she looked at him with her Fay blue eyes that were swollen and red.

"You won't stop killing everyone important to me, will you? WHY CAN'T YOU JUST STOP!?"

Nafury looked to the floor. "If you would have told me that your blood is what he's been using, I could have handled all of this differently."

"I know," Ubi sobbed. "But I didn't want to be your enemy. I didn't want either of you to go to Earth and get hurt. After what they did to Simera—I just couldn't risk losing either of you the same way!"

Nafury looked away from her and down the hall. "Xirel wanted to spend the rest of his life with you and I took him away. That's why you must accept what I have to do next." He got to his feet and started to leave.

"My mother said to leave her world alive!" Ubi screamed at him. She was boiling with rage now. "What will she have left when you resurrect her? Have you thought about that? This is her world! You would return her to a life of nothingness!"

"We are different, Ubi," Nafury replied, pausing in his steps for a moment. "We will not become spirit slaves or be lost to oblivion. Our human bodies are not bound to the Laws of Aragmoth. And both of us owe this world nothing." He continued down the hall.

"That's where you're wrong," Ubi shouted at his back. "We owe this world more than anyone!"

TWENTY-THREE

It was a long flight to the remote volcano island that once was home to most of the griffin shifters on Aster. His mission was made longer when Nafury had to wait on the outside of the volcanic crater. Kenshe had taken to the Keol to travel over, as he would not be seen dead being carried by a dragon.

Nafury pondered just flying up and over to gain entry. But he remembered that Loki had mentioned that Gwa had an unstable mind now. Entering the ruins as the White Death could prove too much for the griffin shifter to handle. He didn't want to break the mind of their one chance to fix the Gate at the Efereal Mountains.

Nafury almost took to the air to try dropping in on the Falls, but Kenshe emerged from the Eternal Waters. He had always been curious to how the phelan managed to pull it off. There were miles of water to swim through for air. All this while under intense the pressure. Then there was how their bodies went from the extreme heat to below freezing temperatures in an instant.

"You sound jealous," Kenshe said. The grizzled-brown phelan dragged himself high up onto the rocks to where Nafury was.

"Hardly."

"When you were Damek, you fashioned the phelan after the first Nightmare Eaters. We are of Aragmoth's being and Thread. Heat and cold don't bother him anymore than it does us. Well, minus when you froze then entire planet over. That was cold enough to feel. Kenshe shook out his fur. Most of the water landed on Nafury.

Nafury let out a long breath, forcing himself to not get mad. Kenshe's sole reason to exist seemed to be to torment him. He needed to accept that and keep his mind on the task at hand, and that was saving Sybl. It was too early in the day to let the phelan get to him. "I must have been drunk back then, as you're still the ugliest thing in existence," Nafury replied.

Kenshe dropped his mind into the past, and tilted his head back as he tried to recall something. "Did we have alcohol back then?"

Nafury sniffled as some of the water tickled his nose, before thinking on it himself. "Yes, we did."

"Huh," Kenshe said and brought his thoughts back. "That sucks. You know, I've been thinking..."

"Oh hell no," Nafury cut him off immediately.

"I was thinking about the differences between phelan and dragons. In many ways, dragons are more real than phelan for the simple fact that dragons were once part Sentry. Sentry are real, while phelan were weaved into being when you were Damek."

"It wasn't that simple," Nafury replied.

"Sure it was. Granted, we were fashioned after the Nightmare Eaters. But ultimately we never came from Earth. We were never real to begin with."

"What are you getting at?"

"I'm thinking of if worst comes to worst and Aster perishes, what happens to us illusions?" Kenshe asked.

"I think you're crazy and drank too much sea water," Nafury replied. "If Aster collapses, you will return to being what you started as. A Nightmare Eater."

"Under Hino's control? I don't think so. We would never answer to Hino," Kenshe stated. "We can't change Gods like the Awls can by simply changing our minds, not when we are pieces of the Great Dragon. If Aster perished, Hino would end up inviting a war onto his world."

Nafury was losing patience talking creation theories with the phelan. "You came with Daath to the first Aster. You were outcasts and demons on Earth, but also part of my—I mean, Daath's army. You were the opposite of Sentry."

"Demons, eh?" Kenshe replied, and looked towards the entrance. "Demons that your sister forgave enough to give souls to. Souls that have survived once before when the worst of the worst hit." He looked at Nafury. "So it would stand to reason that humans and Fay would not be the only ones left if Aster perished. I, for one, would still be there to make every moment of your existence a living Hell."

"How comforting," Nafury replied in a sarcastic tone. He turned his head to the side and brought his sapphire eyes to the sight of the waves crashing up against the rocks.

"At some point or another, and sometime soon, you're going to have to seriously choose a side. I have no intention of destroying Aster against Sybl's wishes. And Gwa in there," Kenshe said as he looked up at the volcano's side that towered over them, "is likely as twisted as you right now in your thinking. I frankly don't care what Gwa wants. But if we are going to get to Earth, we need to side with him long enough to make him fix the Gate. So don't screw this up."

"Whatever, let's just find the loon," Nafury replied.

Kenshe led the way around the volcano to a small cave that looked like it led to the Falls. Nafury followed the phelan shifter until they were forced to unshift in order to continue on. They walked in complete darkness for some minutes until a light at the end of the tunnel came into view.

The once great griffin city they entered was now a shattered remnant of its former glory. The base of the city and volcano that it had been built into was all stone-hard lava. What remained of the Tech and steel walkways overhead now dangled over the city like metal vines. The Falls looked like it had taken a direct hit from the Apocalypse itself. Nafury feared that one of the walkways overhead could come crashing down on them without warning.

"So much science and technology, yet none of it could save them from themselves," Kenshe said, not bothering to look back at Nafury.

"From what I heard, griffins were never ones to share." Nafury stopped walking as what he thought to be a ghost of a griffin appeared at the end of the walkway they were on. The dirty, white and rose-colored feathers of the half cat, half bird indicated that it was Gwa. The griffin took a defensive stance, keeping its eagle-like eyes fixated on Nafury.

"All right, that's enough! Put her down this instant!"

Ubi opened her eyes to what sounded like Prisca

yelling. It took her a moment to realize that she was being carried over one shoulder by a dark-skinned phelan. He was easily the tallest shifter she ever saw. The ayame that chased them were barely half his height as they frantically tried to make him stop.

"I will do no such thing. Now step out of the way," he said with a low, but strong voice.

Ubi didn't have the slightest idea what was going on. She became even more surprised when she saw Loki walking next to them. "Loki?"

"Uh, morning, Ubi." Loki swatted his hand to the right to divert another Thread attack aimed at the phelan shifter. "I found—eh, I mean, he found us."

"Where am I being carried to? And who is he?"

"My name is Jru," the shifter said in introduction as he continued walking through the ayame. "I was your father's mentor all his life."

Ubi's grew wide. She couldn't see his face, but she remembered the shifter who stood next to Kas in her Vision of the past with Vanir. She wondered if she had accidentally summoned her own kidnapper by what she did.

"I apologize for the carryout, but it was proving next to impossible to get an audience with you. That and my Bond has refused to speak to me until I present you to her," Jru said.

"His Bond is a woman from Earth," Loki elaborated.

Ubi hung limp as her mind tried to process it all.

"Jru is also a Master of the Arts," Loki added.

"Arts? Like martial arts?"

Loki swatted another Thread away as he read Ubi's psi. "Yes, something like that. But including aeri and estus energy."

Ubi didn't put up a fight and looked down as Prisca took up Jru's back and was looking furious. "Prisca, it's okay."

"Lord Kenshe left you in my charge! Not this brute's! Ubi, demand that he sets you down at once!"

A devious smile hit Loki's face. "Would you like to be carried as well, Mistress Prisca?"

Prisca lost it on Loki and grabbed all his Threads at once. In one motion, she had Loki crumbling to the floor with a squeak. "I will have you both hung if you so much as raise your voice to her! Do you hear me, Jru?"

"You don't have to worry, Mistress Prisca. We are not so much as leaving the Atrum." Jru came to a stop a few moments later to a room in the lower levels and knocked once before opening it.

"Jru, I made it clear I don't want to so much as —" the dark-skinned woman stopped in her shouting on seeing who he carried.

Jru took it as permission to enter, and set Ubi down on a nearby wooden chair as if she were a new doll to present as a gift.

"By all the gods...she's real."

Ubi kept her cool as the woman rushed towards her, looking her over as if she were some paranormal anomaly.

"She looks like Kas," the woman said with glee. "But those eyes—are they red or blue? Is she truly human?"

"Hello again," Loki said. "This is her lady Ubi, dark Fay and daughter of Asil and Erebus."

Celia hurried from the room and back into it with a panel in her hands. She began to wave it around Ubi, scanning her energy readings. "Unbelievable. She's the exact opposite of Sybl—her estus energy is off the charts." Celia then put the panel down on the table and held out her hand to her. "I'm sorry—I just got crazy excited. My name is Celia. I was also born on Earth. And I see you've done well for yourself, Master Loki." She looked momentarily at the green-haired Awl. "Leader of the Eastern Tribes for that matter."

"I've been doing my best," Loki replied with his most polite tone.

Ubi smiled and took Celia's hand and shook it. "It's nice to meet you. Did you both know my mother as well?"

Jru gave a short laugh as he scratched the back of his head. "We did, and I had the honour of being fired from the Custos by the Caelestis."

Ubi dropped her smile in worry.

Celia laughed. "It was alright. Jru was a Custos at the time and we couldn't be together as long as he was. They are forbidden to take a Bond while serving the Sanctus."

"Oh," Ubi said in understanding. "Like a priest?"

"Yes," Celia replied. "Something like that."

"Sooo, what brought you to Aster, Mrs. Celia?" Ubi asked.

"Oh, stop with the formalities. Last names and addresses like that don't exist on Aster." Celia looked to Jru then. "Could you make us some tea, sweetheart?"

Jru looked instantly relieved to be back in the 'sweetheart' category and not the 'floor mat's.' He headed into the kitchen without hesitation.

"Well, my story starts some time ago I was working for the Falls as a scientist in an establishment on Earth. Long story short, I eventually met Mersael, we fell in love, and I became pregnant with his child. He was a griffin shifter, and heir to the Falls."

"What happened then?" Ubi asked as her curiosity heightened.

"Well..." Celia continued as she took the small plate and cup of tea from Jru. She handed it to Ubi before taking her own."The Falls wasn't going to accept me, or our son as the next in line. The whole half-human thing wasn't going to work with them."

"That's when he tried to kill you and Gwa. By miracle of Aragmoth, I found you near the Gate you escaped through," Jru said, finishing the story. "Then I took you back to the Sanctus. But after the Phoenix destroyed it, we made the Atrum our home."

"That's horrible." Ubi then remembered the talks in the War Room that included the Falls. "Wait, Nafury went to the Falls with Kenshe—will they attack him?"

"There is only one griffin left at the Falls, and that is my son," Celia said. She looked around for another panel stashed in her bookshelf. "He has become dangerous and mad with grief since Sybl's death."

"Gwa hates Nafury more than anything," Jru added and took a step forward in concern. "We need to warn him."

Celia turned on the panel, then tried to get a lock on the Threads that linked it to the Falls. "I just hope we're not too late."

Nafury had only vague memories of the griffins, as they had appeared on Aster after the Last War. The creatures were variations of spirits that came to Aster from Earth, much like Sentry did for dragons, to become the protecting shifts for souls. But their kind was closed off to the rest of Aster and secretive. Most had perished shortly before he broke free of Daath's control. From how the Falls looked now, it was clear that the Great Dragon had caused much of the damage. Gwa was the only griffin Nafury recalled ever seeing up close.

"Long time no see," Kenshe said, trying to break the initial tension between them all.

"Why did you bring that demon here?" Gwa said bitterly as he kept his gaze on Nafury. "Get out of here and take that trash with you."

Nafury peeled the griffin shifter's harsh words off his ego and took a step forward. "We need your help. We have to go to Earth to stop Cirrus."

There was a few moments of silence between them. Then Gwa broke into a sudden and hard laughter that echoed through the Falls.

Nafury, not knowing what to make of the griffin's madness, looked at Kenshe.

"Is this a joke that you can share maybe?" Kenshe asked, also trying to keep his cool against his childhood rival.

"Let me get this straight, you both came here to find a way to get to Earth and stop the Dragon Moon?" Gwa asked, barely able to hold his laughter at bay long enough to speak.

"Yes, and just how—wait, what did you just say?" Kenshe asked.

Gwa shook his head and unshifted in a rush of white mist into his human form. His long, white and rose dreads were a mess and looked like they had been unkept for ages. His face that should have belonged to a man in his twenties looked like a fifty year old. Without saying a word he turned and walked off down the hall.

Kenshe and Nafury followed him. After several turns they reached what looked like Gwa's chosen work room. Pieces of Tech and damaged machinery lay everywhere. Lava had hardened and become a part of the room's walls and windows years ago.

Nafury gave a brief glance around and then looked to the large monitor on the wall in front of the griffin shifter. On it, there appeared a static-covered image of what looked like a mechanical dragon. "Is that him?"

"That there is the end to all our problems," Gwa said, throwing his arms out in the direction of the screen.

"You want Aster to end?" Kenshe asked.

"The Dragon Moon isn't coming for us, you dumb dog. Cirrus' intents are not bent for Aster, but for Earth."

"What? You're not making any sense," Nafury said.

"He's flipping the table for this Apocalypse," Gwa explained. "Once the Dragon Moon devours Aster, he will remake it on Earth. Of course, Earth's current inhabitants will have to be eradicated. With Earth's sun darkened, we will be able to live on. Sybl won't have to be a prisoner and battery for Aster for any longer. Dreams and nightmares can't last or sustain themselves forever, even if she stayed as she is. Sybl will never be able to be alive and real again until this illusion ends and we take over

Earth. That's the driving force behind what Cirrus is doing."

"So Cirrus is destroying the Awls because they're the only ones who can stop him..." Nafury thought aloud. "They're the only ones who can survive on Earth long enough in the sunlight to stop him."

"Sybl said she wanted this Aster to go on," Kenshe added. "This is not one of her wishes. And frankly I don't want to be 'devoured' by anything."

Gwa looked at Nafury. "You spoke with her? When?"

"That doesn't matter," Nafury replied.

"Yes, it matters," Gwa said, getting up from his seat. "Where is she?" He glared at Nafury. "How many times do you plan on killing her!?" Gwa shifted back into his griffin form and sent his talons straight for Nafury. Crushing him against the floor, he opened his beak to strike.

Nafury had to use all his strength to suppress Alexia in him from shifting and tearing the half bird apart.

"Gwa, stop it!"

Everything came to a stop when the voice appeared from the screen. It was followed by the image of a darker woman. She had the same brown eyes as Gwa.

Gwa let go of Nafury and turned to look at the screen, then he sat down like an innocent cat. "Mom?"

"You put your talons down right now before I come over there and beat your ass!" Celia said, with a voice that could shatter concrete.

Gwa started to shake, and several feathers fell from him.

Nafury took the moment to slowly get back to his feet.

"Celia," Kenshe said in surprise.

"I can't believe you would help something like this. Have you forgotten that I'm a human from Earth? Have you forgotten that we too have the right to live? Have you turned into a complete animal!?" Celia scolded Gwa.

"No. Of course not, Mom. I would never let you get hurt."

"Shut up!" Celia shouted at him, and Gwa's long, tufted ears flattened against his head. "You get your ass over to the Efereal Mountains and fix that Gate. And then you are going to shut down this Dragon Moon machine before Hino retaliates and destroys all of us. Have you forgotten Sybl's sacrifice? It's the only thing keeping Hino from destroying all of us right now!"

"She's right," Nafury added. "Hino will not stand aside and let all the humans on Earth perish. I would have sacrificed Aster to save my sister. But if we threaten Earth, Hino will destroy all of us. Sybl will have died for nothing. Then there is no guarantee that this *machine* can bring her back to life."

Gwa was laughing again. "Silly demon. Silly, silly demon in you talking." His brown eyes flashed momentarily, revealing his erratic self. "She always wanted what's best for us, at the cost of her own life. Now it's our turn to give her what's best—and that's a real life, not an imprisonment of death. There is only one way to save the world that I will have any part in, and that's if it includes saving her. Now get out, because I'm not helping you get to Earth." He hit a button on the keyboard and the screen went off.

Nafury looked at Kenshe, with a faint hope that he might help him grab the griffin and go. But Kenshe only crossed his arms in front of him. The phelan looked uncertain to just what he intended to do next. Several buzzing noises pulled Nafury's attention and he looked up. Large guns that had been mounted on the walls were now aiming at them.

"I really hate Tech," Kenshe mumbled as he took a step back and started to retreat.

Nafury looked at all four of the weapons. He started to calculated just how much he could get shot at by them before he would be toast. Alexia was doing the math for him as his fear began to swell up from within him and force him backwards.

TWENTY-FOUR

Everything hurt at once when Nafury opened his eyes sometime later. He was surprised to find that he was still alive and in one piece. "Where am I?"

"Toria," Cecil's voice replied. "Because you're still a complete idiot."

Nafury sat up, feeling groggy as if he had been drugged. "I was still your Prince once. It wouldn't kill you to show some respect, Cecil. How did I get here?"

"Gwa sent you through the Gate. I found you in the basement." Cecil pulled a chair over and sat down, resting his arms on its back.

"Wait, what? You have a working Gate?" Nafury asked in disbelief. Of course Cecil did—he was just as good with Tech as Gwa, just usually without the pieces he needed. Nafury silently cursed himself for not anticipating such. Something dripped from his face and he looked down. A drop of blood had fallen from his nose to his shirt. He wiped his nose with the back of his hand, not knowing what to make of it.

"You really don't know anything. I fixed the one that blew up with the Town of Berion some years ago," Cecil elaborated.

Nafury heard the Town's story from one of the phelan shifters from the Torian Continent a few years ago. The phelan shifter swore in his tale that he saw a kyrie wipe out the Town of Berion with its power. The old timer called it a 'Deathmare.' The tavern in the Harbor called the poor guy insane. Nafury's sister had chosen an interesting creature to speak through, that was for sure. He got a tighter grip on his psi as Cecil was looking at him strangely, as if he were listening in on his thoughts. Cecil had always been smart, but never good with Thread. Now the look in his orange eyes suggested otherwise.

"Don't get all excited," Cecil said and broke their stare-down. "Gwa sent you with a note stuck in your mouth." He lifted the piece of tattered white paper in his hand. It was written with the invisible embroidery that was Thread. "It says that if you try and use the Gate to reach Earth, he'll kill you by cutting the connection from his end."

"I don't need some bird's permission to go to Earth," Nafury spat back and dropped his feet to the floor. His head spun. He didn't have time for a headache now. For some reason, his aeri energy was doing nothing to heal it. He looked around the room and found what else was off. There was almost no Thread present. "Where are the Sentry?"

"We killed them all, after you ran back to the Suzerain Continent." The few Thread present vibrated with estus energy. Cecil was lying. "Look, Nafury," Cecil said and got up from his wood chair, "we all miss her. But you're taking this too far. You will be killed if you go to Earth."

"What are you talking about?" Nafury asked, as every functioning part of his head warned him of where this was going. He looked around for Alexia, but she was nowhere in sight and not answering him.

"Do you take me for an idiot? I know exactly what you will do if you reach Earth and Cirrus. You're a human and your treachery has already proven to have no bounds. You will help him bring your sister back, even at the cost of Aster."

"You're as insane as that damn bird," Nafury said as he tried to get to his feet. He had to sit back down on the bed when the world spun madly.

'Stop dying! They've set a trap for Sybl!'

Nafury looked around the room again, before realizing that Loki was screaming at his psi. "What did you do to me, Cecil?" he asked and looked up at the blue-haired dragoon. Cecil's orange eyes were glowing.

"What's necessary for our survival. Radiation

poisoning is rather rough on humans."

"Why kill me like this? Just to hide the fact that you have already sided with Cirrus?" Nafury asked. This wasn't how he wanted to die. He didn't want to die at all anymore now that he was the only chance of saving Sybl and Aster.

"I don't—"

"You're still a coward that's full of shit!" Nafury said as his anger pushed his adrenaline high enough to empower the balance in his legs.

'Get out of there!' Loki's psi yelled at him again.

He pushed himself past Cecil and towards the door. He had to use the wall to steady himself as he made his way down the hall. By the time he reached the main hall, his sight was almost gone. There was only a blur of dragoons who did nothing but watch their former Prince die before them. No one reached out a hand to help. No one cared. He would never know if they ever did. *Loki...*

"You're living in a world made of nothing but nightmares, human. But there is a way out for you, and that is death," Cecil said as he came up behind Nafury. He kicked him in the back, sending his face into the marble floor.

"Why...do this? Why...if we...are on the same...side?" Nafury asked as he pulled himself in a crawl across the floor. He could feel a faint breeze coming from the main gate. "I want Aster...to remain...as it is."

"It's as I've told you, dumb Prince. Your resolve would never stand up to Cirrus. Everyone knows how close you both were. I'm just guaranteeing the survival of the dragon race. Now that we have Alexia and her power, we only need the last piece. With Sybl contained, this Aster will cease to exist. A new, perfect world without our enemies will arise on Earth," Cecil said.

Nafury didn't have the strength to respond and tell Cecil just how wrong he was. Every former demon that existed now would not just perish.

"I hate to say it, but I've come to the conclusion that we will never be friends. Yet my conscious is clear with the fact that I tried. Goodbye, Nafury."

A clash of steal rang out from the gate, but Nafury was too weak to lift his head to look.

"You monster!" Loki's voice shouted. The Threads that remained trembled as he grabbed the lifelines leading to Cecil. He could only hold them for a moment before one of the High Guard landed a strike to his back. Loki spun around and stabbed his attacker in the chest with a dagger and returned his focus to Nafury. He grabbed him and pulled him over his shoulder and immediately turned to retreat. But before he could shift and run, the main hall roared. The exit was covered with a wall of water, while the room started to flood from Toria's waterfalls.

"This where you get washed out with that garbage

from my castle." Cecil commanded the water against Loki and Nafury. It trapped them in a harsh tornado of water, before flooding them out onto the main gate.

Cecil followed them as his power over water circled him. He began to direct the water to wash them off the side, but a cloaked figure stood at the end of the gate. At their feet was Nafury and Loki. "Who are you?"

"Sentry are not allowed on Aster without Aragmoth's blessing. Neither are their allies." The face lifted, and Sybl's blue eyes glowed a dangerous warning his way.

"There you are!" Cecil shouted, and several Sentry appeared around them. Some were invisibly clinging to the crystal-like walls of the castle. Others emerged from the main hall.

"You sicken me, Cecil. The Laws of Aragmoth demands your death!" Sybl said and the Ain Soph Aur grew brighter and more powerful. In moments its light began to spread from Toria's center and expand towards them in a deafening rush. The Sentry, being unable to fly, were vaporized instantly. Cecil could only shift into his dragon form and flee to avoid being burned alive by its intense energy.

Sybl kneeled down and touched her brother and Loki, just as the light of the Soph Aur washed over them. As she did, the light exploded, releasing a shockwave of aeri energy across Aster.

TWENTY-FIVE

Ubi hit a dead end and looked back before collapsing on the ground in exhaustion. She had lost the army of ayame witches. Relieved, she leaned her back against the wall of the alley to catch her breath. Running wasn't her sport. No sport was her sport unless its reward included over thirty grams of sugar in it to make up for her losses. She had to think and the suffocating air in the Atrum made it impossible. Nafury could be dead right now and it would be all her fault. Loki had left immediately to go help, but the flight over would take him at least a day. If something happened to him, she would never be able to forgive herself. Tears filled her eyes with the thought that she might never see Nafury again. She was destined to be a curse that hurt everyone around her.

She heard footsteps in the snow and looked down the alleyway. She was expecting a street case or an ayame. Instead, there stood a tall and stunningly handsome man. His long, blond hair and watery-blue eyes glowed in the barely-lit alleyway. She recognized him from her Dream with Nafury that it was Cirrus. Now she wanted nothing more than Loki or Kenshe and his ayame to save her hide as she sprung to her feet.

Cirrus stared right at her in a rather still-stiff manner. She froze in fear as she waited patiently for him to make his move first. A gesture, anything that might give a hint of what he might do next.

"You can see me?" he asked in surprise, and he moved closer to her.

"Why wouldn't I see you?" Ubi began to pray that she was just seeing things and that this wasn't Cirrus. His clothes didn't look to be of Asterian design, though. She heard another set of footsteps and looked the other way down the alley. Kenshe jumped down from the rooftop, as agile as a cat.

"I told you not to run away," Kenshe said, clearly irritated.

"Huh? Kenshe?" Ubi asked, then looked at where Cirrus was. She started to back away towards Kenshe, but Cirrus lifted his hands. Silently, the Awl caught the life Threads to the phelan shifter. "How are you back so quick?"

"Stupid pigeon has a Gate. I took the liberty of using it when he opened fire on our asses."

"Where's Nafury?" Ubi asked. She had to know he was still alive.

"He made his own way out," Kenshe answered.

"Tell him to go away or I will kill him," Cirrus warned, and only her ears could hear him.

"Kenshe, stop!" Ubi said as she looked back at the phelan shifter, as it was clear that he couldn't see Cirrus like she could.

Kenshe stopped approaching her, but more out of the fear that resonated from her than by command. He looked around, trying to sense what might have terrified her so. Finding nothing, he tried to look into her psi, but it was completely sealed off. "Ubi, what's wrong?"

She knew that if she screamed for help, Cirrus would kill him. So she turned her fear on him. "I don't want to have anything to do with you anymore! Just get away from me!"

"That's not going to happen. Let's go back to the Atrum. You can finished whining about how you hate everything while there and wait for Nafury to come back." Kenshe took another step forward, but she screamed at him again to stop. "I know you're not scared of me."

"Then you're wrong. Now back—!" Before Ubi could finish, the ground started to shake faster and faster.

Kenshe looked around for just what was causing the earthquake. The Calls were saying that it was coming from Toria. At the same time a shockwave of aeri energy hit Atrum City like a hurricane. He instinctively ran the rest of the way to Ubi, but stopped dead in his tracks when he saw Cirrus standing there. The aeri energy left a sticky glow to his invisible form. "Cirrus?"

"It's been a while, Kenshe," Cirrus replied.

Kenshe took immediate notice of his life Threads in the former dragoon's grasp. There was also a black, twisting Mei on the Awl's arm. Sybl was still Bonded to him. He instinctively charged at Cirrus, brushing Cirrus' pull on his life Threads aside. Colliding with the former dragoon, he pulled them both into the Keol. He struck the former dragoon in the face once on the other side, then backed off from him. He could see that the Mei to Sybl was keeping Cirrus from burning up from the Keol. It was possible that every bit of pain he dealt him was felt by her as well. "What did you do to Sybl? What's happened to you?"

"Ah, Kenshe. Always the faithful one to leave your ayame unattended," Cirrus said cooly.

At Cirrus's words, Kenshe reopened a Rift back to the surface. He shifted and chased after Ubi's scent, landing on her just as a Sentry's scythe-like arm hit. The strike hit him instead, and he let out a yelp of pain. He retaliated and spun around in one swift motion, landing his teeth in the neck of the creature. He tore flesh and bone free of the monster, until it ceased moving.

The Calls for battle were out in force now, and he

could hear his Pack's psi reaching out for him. He picked up Ubi between his teeth, and made a mad dash for the Atrum. Another Sentry nearly pinned his tail to the ground. He jumped up and over one that had been made visible before him, but didn't see the other one in time. It slashed his leg and sent him tumbling in a roll across the street. He shook off the hit, and looked around for where Ubi had landed. He found her unconscious nearby, and quickly unshifted as he gathered her into his arms.

"Where you going, Kenshe?" Cirrus asked as he emerged from his restored invisibility in front of him.

Kenshe set Ubi down and got a grip his own and her life Threads.

"Do you really hope to fight me and win?" Cirrus said as he walked closer.

Cirrus' question was answered when Tank came down on him from an overhead rooftop. The giant phelan shifter grabbed the Awl by the neck, before throwing him across the street.

Kenshe wasted no time using the distraction and grabbed Ubi, pulling them into the Keol. He had to find Sybl before he bled to death, and get her daughter as far away from Cirrus as he could.

Ubi opened her eyes as everything in her body started to hurt at once. She felt as if she had been sunburned three miles from the sun and then rolled across the width of the planet. She rolled to her side and found Kenshe lying down next to her on his stomach. His face was tucked into his arm. A pool of blood around his torso had begun to make its way to where she was for help.

She sat up and tried not to panic as she shook him to wake up. When he didn't respond, she looked around the abandoned building he had brought them too. It took her a moment to realize that they were at the Sanctus, within its lower ruins.

Ubi stood up and looked around for something she could use to slow the bleeding. Everything around her that wasn't solid stone had been reduced to ashes and dust a long time ago. She wondered what kind of a bomb had been set off in her father's temple. "Everyone keeps coming back here," Ubi said as she pulled off her sapphire blue cloak. She tore a strip off of the bottom of it, and the tearing sound cut into her heart and her memories of Xirel. Kneeling next to Kenshe, she tore off what was left of his grey, blood-soaked tunic. Then she started to wrap the blue fabric around him.

"Don't...die..." Kenshe mumbled.

Ubi stopped for a moment. He was talking while unconscious. She touched his wound as the fabric from her cloak began to soak through. His bleeding wouldn't stop. She was sobbing now from fear. Fear of Kenshe dying and leaving her here alone. Fear of dying again and of being completely useless to do anything about it.

"Ubi," a familiar voice called to her. When it registered that it was Cirrus', she sprung to her feet.

She wiped the tears from her face and looked back at Kenshe. She pulled her father's sword from its sheath at his side and lifted it before her.

"Just what do you hope to do with that?" Cirrus' voice sounded amused.

The Awl had a point. Kenshe had only taught her the basics of manipulating Threads beyond magic tricks. She had never used a sword. So she looked for her second weapon of choice. Kenshe's shift moved along the wall like a protective shadow. She called it to her, and it walked over to her outstretched hand. Ubi kept a careful watch for where Cirrus' voice would appear next. How she wished that she could take the phelan's form and kill Cirrus who had taken everything from her.

"You blame me for all the wrong things. I did not take your mother away from you. She would have never have fallen for me if Kas had not abandoned you both to a life of loneliness and suffering."

"So that's supposed to be an excuse for destroying the first Aster and then coming after this one!?"

"What do you care? This is not your world and neither was its previous incarnation. You belong on Earth. We're on the same side and we can help each other, Ubi."

"I'm not helping a delusional freak! You killed Xirel!" Ubi looked back for Kenshe's shift, but the wolf-like creature had disappeared. As her fear rose, so did Cirrus' laughter.

"The phelan shift is far smarter than you are. But I'm not cruel. Come with me quietly and I'll even throw in the extra favour of healing Kenshe there for you. He will continue to bleed and will die if you do nothing."

"You have some nerve to trespass on this sacred ground, Awl!"

Ubi looked back and found Kas standing there. He looked alive and whole.

"I thought you might show up," Cirrus said as he jumped down to the other side of Ubi. She was now in the center of the imminent fight. "After all, Fay don't really die."

"I said to leave!" Kas took his blade from Ubi and pointed it at Cirrus.

"I always wondered if you would have been able to give me a satisfying fight on the beach ten years ago." Cirrus unsheathed his own long sword and aimed it at the dark Fay. "I think I've waited long enough to find out."

Ubi didn't so much as get a blink off when Kas vanished in a swirl of estus energy and reappeared behind

Cirrus. The Awl turned in time to catch the dark Fay's sword against his own. Their steel sung to a quick beat as they continued to battle it out. The ruins of pillars and collapsed walls was now their arena.

Ubi looked back at Kenshe as he still wasn't moving. "Dad, he's going to die!" she said in a whisper of a panic. "How do I get him to safety?"

'Cirrus can only be defeated on Earth. You must go there with Kenshe.'

"Won't he burn up from the sun?" Ubi responded to his psi by voice.

'Not if you Bind him to you. I can feel that you truly love him as he does you. Do not make the same mistake I made with your mother in thinking that such feelings can be pushed aside.'

Ubi couldn't think of anything else she could do to save Kenshe. As the clash of steel drew closer to her again, she rolled Kenshe onto his back and picked up his right wrist. She had no idea how to form such a link to him, especially with him unconscious. Ubi closed her eyes and pressed the back of his hand against her lips, willing the Thread around her to give him to her. Her tears fell to his hand and down his wrist. When she looked at it, she saw several silver Threads begin to grow around her left wrist and his right. She could sense his shift again too, and it made its way back to her.

'Nafury is the only one who can break the Curse that is giving Cirrus his power.' Kas' voice said to her mind.

"He's on Earth too?" A sense of dread filled Ubi, and it seemed to spread as a black hole of a Rift from under her. She gripped Kenshe's hand tight as she let the Rift pull them under to an uncertain destination.

TWENTY-SIX

Several hours later, Nafury opened his eyes as a cold chill stung sharply enough to wake him. He stared up at the blue eyes looking down at him. They were the same colour as Cirrus'.

"You have to get out of here."

"Cirrus?"

"Wake up, now."

Nafury blinked as the room around him began to move faster, blurring out the image of his dead best friend.

"Is he conscious?" a voice asked.

The fog cleared and the light over him became more blinding and revealed the truth of where he was.

"Nothing is working on him. It's as if his body is destroying anything we put into him."

Nafury blinked again and took in a deep breath. The room he was in had a chemical and unnatural smell to it.

"Doctor, what do we do?"

Nafury didn't have an answer for the woman. He looked behind her to where a spirit form of a woman with long, blond hair stood watching him. It wasn't Cirrus here with him, but Alexia. The last thing he remembered was falling into the Soph Aur. *You brought me here?* Nafury asked by psi to Alexia. *I thought Cirrus had captured you.*

'The griffin was able to disable me and push me through the Gate to Earth. I am captured by no one unless I wish it. You landed rather rough and I had no choice but to let them bring you here until you recovered.'

"Earth?" Nafury asked aloud and sat up, before looking at his arms and chest where several wires had been hooked up to him. So he had made it.

"Yeah, welcome back to it," one the white-dressed workers said to him. Then he pushed him back down.

Nafury found the man's words ironic. The last time he was on Earth he had almost destroyed the whole planet. He pulled the wires off of himself and started to get to his feet. The doctors backed off when he struck their hands away and started to call for security.

Alexia silenced them by pulling all the air from their lungs. The doctors were left gasping and fleeing into the hallway for air.

Sybl didn't save his life so he could cause havoc on Earth all over again, and he called Alexia's attack off. Nafury knew that he was pushing his luck with how far he could harm the humans before Hino retaliated. Even if there was no guessing to how long it would take the One God's Sentries to try and kill him.

He sensed more trouble coming from the voices at the end of the hall and Alexia's energy began to rise in response. In the time it took him to blink his eyes, people were blown against the surrounding walls with a vengeance when they entered the room. They were then held there by Alexia's intense wind.

The shouting in the room became chaotic and he looked at the nurse that had moments ago been looking down at him. She sat shaking against the wall of the hospital, a smear of blood behind her. He crouched down in front of her and the woman trembled. Nafury wondered if this was how so many had been terrified of him once. It was a sad kind of irony, as he had always hated his adoptive father for instilling fear on others. Now, he had become just like Simera. He reached out to the woman and used his aeri to heal the wound on the back of her head.

She seemed to have some idea of what he did as she reached to where he had touched her and found that the wound was now closed. "What are you? Some kind of wizard?"

"No," Nafury replied, wiping the blood from his hand onto his black pants. "Wizards are imaginary, but dragons are real." Standing up straight, he looked to a nearby window. He opened it and looked down to the busy city street twenty stories below, before stepping off of the ledge.

Atrum City was in chaos when Sybl emerged from the Gate and left the black castle. The aeri still stuck to the Sentry and made them visible, but they were outnumbering the phelan shifters in the streets. She walked with her festra in hand for the first one she saw, and made sure that it saw her in turn. It was enough to get all their attention, as the giant, insect-like creatures were all connected to one another. She swiftly cut down the Sentry focused on her, then took to the rooftops as she sung her song of death, and trailed one attacker behind her. It made her presence known, and the Sentry were agitated by the aeri pulsing now through the Animus Threads, which betrayed their invisibility even more. Sybl wasted no time going for the next one as it joined her on the rooftop and cut its legs out from under it. The Sentry fell helplessly into the waiting teeth below.

All Calls ceased for mere moments, as Prisca reorganized the song of death. Only the Caelestis had ever sung it.

She could see Sybl from the window of the Atrum, as she attacked non-stop the Sentry with her festra and aeri. Sybl was luring them away from the City and into the fields. *Assist your Caelestis! Don't let them capture her!*

The Packs re-synced with their ayames, as the song of death continued. They immediately turned their focus and energies to pulling the Sentry off of Sybl's tail.

Sybl held her own against the Sentry, as she sent several flares of aeri energy back at her pain train. The ones she hit dead on were vaporized, and any nearby were blinded. She knew she had only so much energy to get this done. The phelan assisted her in tearing asunder the ones temporarily blinded. They ganged up on the bigger, more dangerous of the Sentry by instinct and experience, and made quick work of the creatures.

Blood covered the field as the slaughter continued. Sybl's bladed festra didn't slow as it cut down the enemy in a flurry that lasted for thirty minutes. Finally, the phelan overwhelmed the last Sentry and the fight was over. Many of the Sentry corpses remained, as the estus energy in the air didn't allow their bodies to turn into stardust.

Sybl was spent as she collapsed to one knee. She held onto her festra that she stuck upright in the ground to keep herself from toppling over.

"Sybl!" Feryl's voice said and he unshifted as he ran to

her. "Are you hurt?"

"Just a bit...tired," Sybl replied and pulled herself to her feet. As she did, the Call went out that the Sentry were all dead. Cheers erupted from the phelan and they unshifted in their own exhaustion. The entirety of the massacre strewn around them made for an unbelievable sight.

"Well, that went a lot better than expected. I feel like kicking myself for not believing Nafury that you were back," Feryl said as he looked at his Pack. They were equally happy to see the Caelestis again.

"It's not over yet," Tank said as he pointed to someone behind Sybl.

Sybl turned around and saw Cirrus walking over to them. The shifters took in hand their blades at the sight of the Awl, as others shifted and flared their teeth in warning. But the Awl wasn't alone, as Cirrus dragged and held Loki hostage in the grip of his arm. "Let him go you bastard!"

"I will, as soon as you give up this pointless fight and come with me," Cirrus replied.

"I will not let you kill anyone else who is important to me!" Sybl snapped back and got a grip of Loki's Threads. She pulled her hand back, and Loki vanished in a blink of stars. In a heartbeat, he reappeared under her hand, whole again.

"That was...scary," Loki said as he regained himself

and started looking for Cirrus' Threads.

"Impressive, Sybl. Or with the presentation of your latest remembered powers, should I call you Asteria?" Cirrus taunted.

Sybl lifted her Cursed arm as she tried to resist the control he tried to force over her.

"You cannot resist," Cirrus said and cut the Threads to one of her legs, causing her to collapse. "You belong entirely to me!"

Loki retaliated as he snapped the control to Cirrus' arm, then sent one of his daggers for the Awl's heart. But Cirrus caught the weapon before it could hit its mark with his other hand.

Sybl picked up her festra as she channeled Sial's power over Gravity under Cirrus. "I've had about all I can stomach of you. Begone!"

The ground exploded and hurled Cirrus into the air. Loki swiftly grabbed every Thread he could of the Threads to the Awl. He snapped them, but just as he did, Cirrus vanished into thin air.

"Is he dead?" Feryl asked as he looked everywhere.

"I can't kill him as long as he Bonded to Sybl," Loki said and looked to Sybl. The black Thread of the Bond to Cirrus was still on her wrist.

"You cannot defeat me," Cirrus said. The Packs scrambled to try and find him.

"Sybl, can you Nova him out?" Loki asked.

"He's holding my voice," she said as she collapsed to her knees. She raised her festra, just as a scythe-like arm came down on her.

"I've played long enough with you," Cirrus said. He pulled back and tore her festra from her hands, throwing it across the field.

Before anyone could react, his other arm swept them across the field. Then Cirrus pulled Sybl into his invisibility.

"Sybl!" Loki shouted as he tried to grab a Thread—any that led to her or Cirrus, but they had all vanished. "Sybl, no! Bring her back!" He collapsed to his hands in tears as there was no way to follow as he couldn't see them or their Threads.

Prisca caught up to them and looked every which way for Sybl. "Where is the Caelestis?"

Feryl had just peeled himself off the ground. He bled from the scythe having cut his chest.

"Where is she!? Sybl was just here—where did she go?" Prisca demanded. She struck Feryl hard across the face, and he landed on his backside.

"He took her," was all Feryl could say in reply, uncaring to the blood that trickled from his mouth.

She then went straight for Loki. "Why didn't you protect her!?"

Loki said nothing as Prisca grabbed him by his shirt and lifted him off of the ground. When she didn't get an answer, she threw him back down.

Prisca paced about for a moment, before looking back at Loki. "We are going after her—but I need to know when it's sunset on Earth. Can tell me that at least you useless dragon Awl!?" Prisca shouted at him.

Loki came around enough to understand what she was saying. He quickly tapped into the other Awl's psis. "Two hours. It goes down in two hours our time."

"Then we don't have much time," Prisca said and looked around. She turned to the Packs who stood on the field. "Seven alphas and two more ayame are coming with me to Earth through the Atrum's Gate. We are bringing Sybl back. If anything gets in our way of that, then we will reduce it to what lies on this field right now."

"Lady Prisca, Earth's sun will kill us if we can't get back in time," one of the alphas spoke.

"Then you will die and be remembered by Aragmoth when he reincarnates you on Aster. But there will be no Aster left if we don't get the Goddess back! I will hear no excuses or cowardice—get yourselves together, right now! That's an order!"

The Packs consulted amongst themselves as they chose their strongest and smartest alphas. Within minutes, the six chosen from the ranks stepped forward.

Feyrl and Tank were locked in disagreement of who should go.

"Speed won't be of much use on Earth. We're going to

have to intimidate the shit out of them before they can open fire on us," Feryl said.

"Are you sure, Feryl?" Tank said as he briefly looked at Prisca who had no patience left in her. "Fine. It's better if I'm there if things go wrong. You still have some years left in you."

"Dad, are you sure?" Prisca asked, in concern of his age.

"I couldn't save Sybl's mother from Simera. But I'll be damned before I meet my death having failed to save her daughter. I'm going, and that's final. With some luck, Boss will be watching over us on Earth and make sure we don't get turned into ashes."

Feryl patted Tank on the back, before looking to the leftovers of the Packs. The task of cleanup before the bodies of the Sentry could start to rot was left to them.

TWENTY-SEVEN

Kenshe didn't know how he got to where he was now, but that wasn't enough to make him wake Ubi. Not even as Earth's sun began to rise in the horizon and creep its light into the room of the tower they were in. It was a magnificent sight, and it should have burned him to ashes. But as the rays passed his knees and rose to cover him completely, he remained alive.

He looked at the Aliyr on his wrist that bound him to Ubi and let out a sigh of relief. Being Bonded to a Fay had its advantages. He had not only survived sunrise on Earth, but he had healed and never felt stronger. His other half, however, was completely out cold.

Kenshe went over to the bed and contemplated waking her up. He was completely lost with just what was going on and what they were to do next.

Kenshe lowered his head and closed his eyes. He had

to think straight. He had seen Sybl's memories before—all he had to do was remember her memories of Earth. He hated Tech, but he had to make it work in his favour while he was here. He opened his eyes and turned around, and found the thing with a screen that they called a TV. He went over to it and examined its buttons. Picking the one that could only be red as his eyes couldn't pin a colour to it, he pushed it. There was a beep and the machine came on.

...in the unveiling of the latest weapon to combat extraterrestrials, its founder was nowhere to be seen today. There have been ongoing speculations of his health, and as our financial advisor...

Kenshe stepped back from the images, realizing that they were talking about Cirrus. The former dragoon had staged his workings here as a weapon against the Asterians. He wouldn't be surprised if forcing them to Earth was all part of his plan too. If they performed as dangerous invaders, he would win the humans' trust by killing them. Then he would likely strike the humans with their defences down.

"Kas said it was a Curse allowing him do this," Ubi said as she sat up and rubbed her eyes.

"Curse? Please don't tell me you mean *that* Curse. I thought it was destroyed with Daath and Moon."

Ubi shook her head. "Cirrus and my mother have it now."

"And wait, you saw Kas again?" Kenshe asked.

"He sent us here from the Sanctus you collapsed in. He held off Cirrus and opened a Rift under us."

Kenshe's spirits perked up at the thought of his best friend being alive. "Alright, so how do we get rid of this Curse once and for all?"

"He said that Nafury is the only one who can break it and that he's here already," Ubi replied.

Kenshe's enthusiastic expression fell through the floor. "Just great. Leave the Fate of two worlds to the one who nearly destroyed them." He sat down on the sofa next to her.

"Can you find him? Sniff him out or something?"

"Finding him, even on this world, won't be a problem. But after watching that woman on the screen just now, everything screams a trap. And then there's this," Kenshe said, holding up his wrist. "You even know what this is?"

"No idea," Ubi replied. "It just happened and then worked in keeping you alive so far. The sunlight and Sentry won't bother you as much with that leash—eh, I mean, mark on you."

"No, you had it right the first time," Kenshe said. "It's a bloody leash. A leash that says you're my mate."

Ubi's face went completely red. "Well, then just take it off if it bothers you so much. I think I have a dustpan in the closet if you turn to ashes..."

The side of Kenshe's mouth involuntarily twitched. He

was going about this the wrong way. Then it occurred to him that they were in her home on Earth, not some random place. "This is your place?"

"Yeah," Ubi said and got up and stretched. "Simera's apartment is just down the hall if you don't believe me."

Kenshe's curiosity was uncontainable.

"Key is hanging next to the door. I'm going to make me some coffee," Ubi said with a yawn. She headed then towards what looked like a Tech-inspired kitchen.

Kenshe let his senses tour the apartment first before he went for the key. He picked it off the hook and opened the door, and walked towards the last apartment at the end of the hall. The key worked, and he cautiously opened the door. He was walking into a dragon's den, even if that dragon was now dead. At first he thought that he had the wrong apartment, as the place had clearly benefitted from a feminine touch. The flowers had wilted in their vase on the dining table, but for the most part, the place was clean. He went into the living room and looked at several pictures in their frames on the shelf. The women in one looked a lot like Sybl. He wondered if Simera had taken refuge at Serena's old place while he was trapped here on Earth. He picked up the photo and pulled it out of the frame, looking for a name on the back.

"It says—"

"'Best friends forever.' I can read English," Kenshe said.

Ubi shrugged him off and came the rest of the way in, before sitting down on the sofa. She looked to be enjoying her cup of coffee.

Kenshe looked closer at the blond woman in the photo. It was a more human-looking Alexia. "Some best friend," he commented bitterly. "Alexia nearly killed Sybl." He put the photo into his pocket. Kenshe went over to the closet then. He started to unwrap the piece of Ubi's cloak that she had used to bandage his chest. Then he picked out the least dragon-smelling shirt, which was a formal grey one.

"Why would she pretend to be human at all?" Ubi pondered aloud. "Serena isn't the reincarnation of anyone. Sure, she went on to be Queen of Toria, but she's just human," Ubi said.

"She was more than that. She could see into the future from what I was told. A very useful talent if you ask me, especially as Awls stayed far from dragons back then. Alexia probably wanted to capitalize on it, as she remained a Sentry," Kenshe replied.

"Maybe," Ubi said and took another sip of her coffee.

"Did he take care of you?" Kenshe dared to ask as he went over to her, buttoning the last of his shirt before sitting down.

"If a prisoner can be seen as cared for. He owns this whole building. That's how I was able to get the guards to help me drag your unconscious butt up here."

"Was Simera in on all of what Cirrus is doing?"

"I think he tried to stop him, by human rules that is. When he failed, he came back here under Cirrus' control. I didn't know who or what had taken control of Simera at the time. All I remember is running for my life when he looked at me with different eyes and tried to grab me."

"That's when Xirel found you?"

Ubi nodded.

Kenshe let out a long sigh and leaned back on the sofa. He held out the piece of cloak he still held, covered in his blood and all. "I can never replace him." He set the fabric down on her lap. "At best I can make you forget him, if only for a while. That's all I can promise."

"I thought you were taking the Bond off?" Ubi asked.

"It's not something that can be removed unless both sides want it to be. It's not something that can be made, either, unless both sides share the same feelings."

"If that's true, then what did you get from being so mean to me?" Ubi asked as she picked up the piece of her cloak.

"Because you're Kas' daughter, in another life or whatever. I couldn't do anything when he died—his strength just gave out and I never forgave myself for that. Every time I look at you, I'm reminded of how I couldn't save him. Pushing you away was how I dealt with it. For what it's worth, I'm sorry."

"It's fine. I had a feeling my presence hit some kind of

angry personal note with you." She traced the Threads of the Mei on her wrist, looking for anything else she may have missed of Kenshe.

"You almost had my own shift kill me when we first met."

"You had strung Xirel up like a piece of meat!" Ubi retorted.

"That was between me and him. And then there was your deception to get closer to all of us."

"I had every right to be cautious, if not superficial. I haven't had it easy, and I didn't want to try surviving on another world by myself," Ubi replied.

"Fine. Just make sure you apologize to Nafury when we see him then."

"Since when do you care about him?"

Kenshe leaned forward and rested his arms on his legs. "The only reason he's alive is because I ordered no one to touch him. He hasn't survived the last ten years by luck."

"That's not answering the question," Ubi said.

Kenshe interlocked his fingers as he thought over his next choice of words. "There is another history between us, from another life. That's all."

Ubi raised an eyebrow. "Who were you before this?"

"Svarog."

Ubi nearly spat out her coffee, and instead choked when she tried to keep it in. "No friggin way. Dragons aren't reborn as phelan. Bull shit."

"Well, that's what happened."

"Okay, well Damek existed during the Last War. Dragons... Not so much."

"We were alive and a prisoner like you were here," Kenshe said, looking around the room. "Nephena wouldn't let us out of the bowels of Toria. Likewise, Tenu wouldn't let her dragons out of the Eternal Waters. But we saw everything."

"Svarog... Wait, the first blacksmith dragon, right?"

"Yeah," Kenshe said and got to his feet. "And I think we should stop lounging around now and go find my helmet."

TWENTY-EIGHT

"Well well, lookey here. The last of the Four Generals to be found in the sewers of Hell, covered in shit."

Nafury opened his eyes and looked up at the man who looked like Kenshe. "Who are you?"

"Your favourite Nemesis, of course. The one who usually ends up bailing you out of the shit you fall into."

"Kenshe...? What are you doing here? And why are your eyes red?" Nafury asked, sitting up taller.

Kenshe took Nafury's hand and pulled him to his feet. Then he went over to the water that flowed through the smelly sewers to take in his reflection. Instead of grey, his eyes were indeed red. "Weird."

"What are you doing here?" Nafury asked, and looked then at Ubi as she charged at him with a hug.

"Saving you! I thought that griffin had killed you!" she replied and hugged him tighter.

Nafury hugged her back, whispering a prayer in thanks that she was safe. "You shouldn't be here—it's too dangerous."

"Yeah, well it can't be worse than Atrum City right now. The Sentry have overtaken it and nearly gutted us," Kenshe added.

"What?" Nafury said. "Then we only have so much time to take out the Dragon Moon while they're busy there."

Kenshe started forward, in the direction he smelled a lot of griffins. "I think I have an idea of where the pigeons flew off too as well."

"Wait, how did you find me so fast?" Nafury asked as he followed after him with Ubi behind.

"Your helmet. It's how I've been able to keep tabs on you."

"Wait, what?" Nafury asked and took his helmet off. They climbed out of the sewers then and into a small, greener area of the city.

"I made that helmet. It was supposed to be a gift for you. I and several other dragoons wanted to join your side during the Last War. We wanted revenge against the chimeras who had imprisoned us."

"You were a dragoon once? I don't believe it," Nafury replied.

"I was the first one, Svarog," Kenshe corrected. "Because I made that helmet with my own hands, it was effortless for me to track the Threads to its gold."

"A gift? For me? I'm touched. Give me a second to puke," Nafury said as they walked along the sidewalk, trying to blend in as best they could.

"You were more admirable when you were Damek. Now you're just an idiot," Kenshe replied bluntly.

"Why the hell are you here again?" Nafury asked and then looked at Ubi who was giggling behind them.

"You both look like you just walked out of a dragon cosplay convention." Ubi was laughing harder now.

"What is that?" Nafury asked.

Kenshe used his Aliyr to see what she was comparing them to. "It's a get together of lots of people where they mock dragons for several days."

Nafury didn't know how they had both become so in sync with each other, until he saw the Aliyr on Kenshe's wrist. He stopped walking so fast, Ubi's nose smashed into his back with a squeak. "Just what is that?"

"Ah...crap. If it's of any consolation, I didn't—" Kenshe didn't get to finish his sentence as Nafury's fist went straight into his face. It hit him hard enough to floor him. Then the phelan shifter caught the boot that nearly stepped on him next. "Will you let me explain!?"

"I will not have some dog with my niece. Release the Bond you have to her at once!"

"Stop it already! You're going to get us killed if you draw anymore attention our way!" Kenshe yelled at him, as his eyes caught the glimmer of a Sentry on a rooftop.

"I'm not the one who has to worry the most about the Sentry, phelan. I should let them cut you to pieces!" Nafury shouted at him.

"I get that you're angry — but if you hurt me, she will feel it too!"

Nafury had forgotten how Bonds worked. He looked at Ubi who was rubbing her sore cheek — the same spot his fist had collided with Kenshe.

"Ow. Can you both stop it now?" she asked.

Nafury took back his boot. "Sorry, Ubi," he said and gently touched her cheek, using his aeri to heal the hit. Then he turned back around and grabbed Kenshe by his shirt and lifted him to his feet. "We'll take this up later." He pressed forward then to the dragon-shaped building that could be seen in the distance.

After a while they reached the Dragon Moon, and it was intimidating. It sat like a mother dragon with its wings covering its fledgling humans underneath. It was nearly all polished metal and glass, as its edges reflected the sunlight in all directions. Yet it was all arranged in such a manner that it almost appeared alive.

Kenshe and Nafury both looked back as their shifts kept their distance from the Dragon Moon. Humans walked about and through the spirits, oblivious to their invisible presence.

"Looks like we go on without them," Kenshe said as he started for the entrance.

"You can't just go through the front doors like that!" Ubi said and chased after them.

"That's exactly what we're going to do," Nafury said putting his helmet back on. He unsheathed his blade as Kenshe did the same.

"They'll gun us down!" Ubi cried.

"Don't kill any, Kenshe. Our success depends on beating this thing before Hino decides to beat us."

"We won't have to worry about that." Kenshe looked to where the griffin shifter standing guard took notice of them. "We're just here to cull the pigeon population." Kenshe moved faster than lightning, as he charged the griffin shifter. He cut him down before the guard could reach the trigger on his gun. Nafury did the same to the second, only a moment slower. The alarms went off as they entered through the front doors, and security guards began to fill into the front foyer. Then they opened fire on them.

Ubi took cover behind the front desk. Kenshe and Nafury continued to slaughter the griffin shifters who couldn't aim fast enough. She dared to peek up at the computer where she was. She let her power search through its information to find just what part of the Dragon Moon they had to hit. Once she had the answers she needed, she used her power over it to make the lights go out.

Alexia's power still reached Nafury, and his eyes quickly adjusted to the dark. The griffin shifters scrambled to adjust their helmets, only to be cut down before they could.

Ubi ran to them when it was clear, and then to the elevator they needed. "Fifteenth floor. If I can get my hands on the main generator, we can blow this dragon to the moon."

"Sounds like a plan," Kenshe said as the elevator arrived with a ding. They went inside and the door closed before starting upwards. "I know this is a bad time in our relationship to ask for a favour," Kenshe started as he looked at Nafury. "But could I borrow your wings once this place blows?"

"Like how you left me to die at the Falls?" Nafury replied with a cold tone.

"Hey, I did what I could, you unappreciative prick!"

"Like hell you did," Nafury replied, unconvinced.

"Nafury..." Ubi whined.

"Fine," Nafury said, looking briefly back at Ubi. "But only so I can drop your Bond from space so he can become a stain on the ground that you won't feel."

"Come on, Nafury," Kenshe replied, pretending to whine. "We are supposed to die with a death grip to each other's throats as we tumble into Hell. You are ruining the foundation of our friendship."

"You guys are pathetic," Ubi said as she hid to the side of the elevator as the doors opened. They were greeted with another group of soldiers. Kenshe and Nafury followed Ubi's lead as they were opened fire on.

"Shit, these ones are human," Kenshe said as he looked at Nafury.

"Yeah, I'm on it," Nafury said as he focused his psi on the weak human minds attacking them. He gave their heads the illusion that they were being charged at. While their guns pointed the other way towards the illusions, Kenshe and Nafury struck them down from behind. One of Kenshe's blades hit a little too deep, and a spark of electricity from an overhead light ignited. It was a warning from a Sentry.

Nafury kneeled down and healed the human just enough that he would live. Then they continued forward. "Can you be more careful?"

"My bad," Kenshe admitted and looked back to check on Ubi who stayed close to them.

"There," she said, running to the metal doors ahead.

"Can you open it?" Nafury asked.

"I can try." She set her hands on the control panel and focused on wrecking the circuitry. It worked, and the doors opened a few inches.

Kenshe grabbed one side, while Nafury did the other and they pulled it open the rest of the way. Kenshe went in first, and gave a quick look around to find that no one was inside.

Nafury and Ubi followed him, and they went for the giant Tech in the center of the room.

"There aren't any windows," Kenshe took immediate notice of.

"I have two eyes," Nafury reminded him and looked over the contraption. He peered through its small window and had to look twice to confirm what he saw.

"Congratulations on getting here late," Cirrus' voice said from the only way into the room.

"What have you done to my sister!?" Nafury demanded.

"I'm afraid you still aren't seeing the whole picture, my Prince," Cirrus replied. "When the first Aster was destroyed, Asteria was not destroyed with it. She merged her essence into her daughter, which is why Asil lived and Erebus did not. Within that tank is the most powerful life-giving force in the universe, next to Hino himself. With that power I will recreate the first Aster here, and Sybl will be alive as she was always meant to be."

"Release her! This is madness you're attempting!" Kenshe shouted at him.

"It will all be over soon," Cirrus said and used his Mei to channel his will to Sybl. The dragon-shaped construct shook as it came alive and began to stand up.

"Nafury!" Ubi pleaded, as Kenshe charged for Cirrus with his blade. "You have to stop him! You're the only one who can!"

Nafury desperately searched for a way to stop Cirrus. He felt completely helpless. Kenshe held Cirrus off, relying on him to think their way out of this. It was then that he caught sight of the Mei mark on Ubi's wrist. "Those are unbreakable..." Nafury thought aloud. He went over to the tank that immersed Sybl's unconscious body in golden water. "You belong to me," he said and pressed his head and hand against the window. "You have always belonged to me, my most precious Fay."

The shaking stopped, and Cirrus grabbed Kenshe and threw him to the side on realizing what was happening. The Awl charged at Nafury, and he caught Cirrus' blade against his own. The Awl's strength pressed him against the tank. "You promised me once that you would never leave me. But you lied—I have never seen you further from what we had once hoped for together!"

"Why can't you see that I do this for us and for Sybl—and for the greater of all Asterians?" Cirrus said.

"You will never create a perfect Aster from suffering!" Nafury shouted back, and pushed Cirrus' blade off and away from him.

Kenshe slashed at Cirrus from behind, and Nafury got a firm grip on his blade to assist the phelan shifter.

Ubi focused on trying to free Sybl from the metal prison. She hit everything, and it was enough as it opened and spilled a flood of water across the room. She grabbed Sybl before she could go with the water closer to the fight. "Mom! Mom wake up! We need your help!" Ubi shook her till she opened her eyes.

Sybl took notice of Ubi, then of the fight at the other side of the room. She pulled herself to her feet, channeling all of her aeri to her as she did. "Kenshe!"

Kenshe heard her thoughts and unleashed a flare of estus energy at Cirrus. He grabbed Nafury and pulled them to the ground as Sybl's aeri hit the Awl immediately after, resulting in a massive explosion. When the energy and debris cleared, Cirrus had vanished.

Ubi let out a breath of relief, and ran over to Kenshe and Nafury as they rolled over in pain. Kenshe had taken most of the hit from the blast for them both.

"Sister..." Nafury started, with the wind knocked out of him.

"We have to go," Sybl replied and pulled him to his feet. "We don't want to be in here when it blows up."

TWENTY-NINE

They followed after Sybl as the Dragon Moon shook violently. Once they were outside, Alexia and Kenshe's shift rejoined with them. Now it wasn't just the Dragon Moon they had to worry about, but the military fully armed and ready to shoot them down. Several tanks stood in the way of their retreat. Ubi looked up as a helicopter blinded them with a spotlight from above. They were completely surrounded.

"Oh no, not this again," Nafury said as he took up position in front of Sybl. "Please tell me you have a plan?"

"Yeah, we have our own Tank," she said and nodded in the direction of the military.

Several large black shapes emerged from the shadows, in a chorus of low growls. The military froze as the massive wolf-like creatures surrounded them. One of the giant wolves fearlessly walked right through their center.

"Hold your fire!" the lead officer ordered, then looked back at the entourage in front of the building. "Who are you and what do you want?"

"We retrieved our kind and just want to go home, General Ray," Sybl called back. She had read everything she needed to know from his defenseless mind. "We have no conflict with anyone else on Earth or any wish to hurt anyone."

Tank feared none of the guns and machinery as he walked over to them, pushing aside a car with his paw like it were a mere toy. "Caelestis, we have come to escort you," he said in English. His voice caused several of the soldiers to soil themselves.

Sybl smiled and looked back at General Ray. "We will be leaving now, is that alright with you?"

The growls became lower, challenging the General to say no. He couldn't say no, as his men would be slaughtered.

Nafury helped his sister by using his own psi to increase the General's fear of them. When Kenshe saw what he was doing, he did the same and a mischievous grin grew on his face.

The General nodded after some minutes, and Sybl let Nafury pull her into his shift. Kenshe pulled Ubi onto his back and shifted, and they followed their escort towards the Gate.

The phelan moved through the streets like shadows.

Traffic and people stopped and screamed in terror as they passed. Many had taken refuge in their vehicles.

"Maybe I should have let Feryl come instead," Tank said to Prisca as they raced the last few blocks for the Gate. "He would have loved to have seen this all again."

Ubi hung on tight with one hand, as she reached down to grab a cellphone from an unsuspecting man. Her victim had been too engrossed with it to notice the wolves till they had already passed him. "Souvenir, check."

"Ubi," Nafury said as he dove closer to them.

"On it," Ubi said and she turned around on Kenshe. She focused back on the Dragon Moon and visualized the controls she had seen. Remembering the connections, she focused her power to set it to explode. It erupted into the sky as the cries of fear echoed as far as they were now. "I hope that didn't hit anyone important..." Ubi turned back around on hearing what sounded like a fight up ahead.

"Master Gei!" Kenshe said ecstatic and rushed ahead on seeing the Iynx. He skid to a stop before the human form that the once cat-shaped General had taken to. Gei's short blond hair sparkled, as his green eyes glowed from the face of man who looked anything but thousands of years old.

"Holy cheese he's pretty," Ubi said first, and Kenshe's fur stood slightly on end.

"I have ensured that this Gate will take you back home," Gei said as he released the dead griffin shifter from his grip. He then looked to Nafury as the dragon landed.

Nafury unshifted to let Sybl see him for herself.

"You found your wings," Sybl said as she stood up straight and walked closer to Gei. It made a sad kind of sense why Gei had torn them off to begin with—any woman would have been instantly taken by him. "Will you not come back with us?"

"Cirrus must answer for his crimes, as Hino has his Laws as well," Gei explained.

"We've missed you," Kenshe said.

"You will be fine without me. I have taught you everything I know. Now hurry, all of you. You must pass through the Gate before they are able to close it again."

Kenshe unshifted and proceeded through the Gate's watery portal, and the others followed.

Nafury stayed another moment behind. "Gei."

"Damek," Gei replied. "I'm happy to see that you've come to your senses."

"Heh, I just wish I did sooner. Will you be alright on your own here?"

"I can hold my own," Gei assured him. "You and the other Generals have babied me long enough."

Nafury laughed as some memories returned from ages past. They did used to overprotect him, but that was only because he was too trusting and timid.

"We are the only two left of the once renowned Four Generals, but it is enough to get done what needs to be done. I am far more concerned with you and the possible futures I have foreseen."

"Oh?" Nafury asked in concern.

"Do not let your wishes from the past consume you in the present. You must let go what must be let go if there is to be peace on Aster."

"I don't understand," Nafury replied.

Gei looked at Nafury's wrist. "You understand exactly what my words are conveying to you. Now you just need the strength to see that the peace we have obtained today is not undone."

Nafury looked at his wrist, before looking back at Gei. The General had shape-shifted into his slender, cat-like appearance, and his white fur glowed. "What if I don't want to?"

"There are consequences to every action," Gei replied. "If you defy the dark Fay, he will have his vengeance. With his strength returned to him from Aragmoth, he may very well obtain it."

Nafury set his arm back at his side and started for the Gate. "Will you help me if it comes to that?"

"We exist to serve the Caelestis' wishes. She is all we have left of Asteria now, and she is all that we need to define our existence. Just do not do anything rash," Gei said. "I have raised and loved Kas like my own son. I will not assist you in destroying him." He then turned and jogged off into the trees as several sirens could be heard coming closer.

Nafury committed his words to memory, then stepped through the Gate. He wanted to keep his sister safe and at his side. Any and all possible consequences of pursuing his wish fell on deaf ears.

GLOSSARY

Aeger — The Sylvan Aur is the equilibrium for the aeri and estus Aurs, creating a balance of life and death energy over the world of Aster. When the Sylvan Aur was destroyed at the end of the Last War, this balance was lost, and the estus energy began to spread uncontrollably across the world. The Aeger is a sickness caused by being overwhelmed by estus energy and its related emotions. Those with the Aeger usually lose their minds before they die of starvation, injuries as they don't feel pain, or they are destroyed. When the Sylvan Aur was restored after Sybl's death, the Aeger ceased to be.

Aeri — Light energy channelled easiest through Animus Threads by positive emotions such as love, happiness and contentment. Used best as a restorative healing energy, but can be channelled into an intense, pure fire that is most effective against those infused with estus energy.

Alexia — Originally believed to be a human woman from Earth who Dyaus caught after venturing through a Gate from Mer City to Earth. She later becomes Cirrus' mother and Dyaus' Bond. Once loved and remembered by the dragons for her beauty, foresight and singing voice.

She lives on as her original form now, as an unusually powerful Sentry from Earth.

Aliyr — Twins on the first Aster were born as a Mei (shield) and an Aliyr (sword). Usually it was the male of the twins if one is a boy and the other a girl. In the case of Bonds on the new Aster, it is usually the male.

Animus — Also known as 'Thread,' it serves as connecting lines for telepathy, shifting, and can be manipulated by estus and aeri energies to heal or destroy amongst many things. It's an endless weave of spiritual links that can only be seen in a trance, by trained Novaists or Callers, Awls, or by those who are connected to the inner realm of death and Aragmoth.

Aragmoth — The immense, living essence that supports the world of Aster. The first Aster was destroyed by a moon-size monster of energy, known as the Dragon Moon, that was sent by Earth. After the destruction of their world, the Eminor spirits combined their energies and Aragmoth was formed. Aragmoth defeated the Dragon Moon and absorbed its dark energy into itself and hurled the Dragon Moon's light essence back to Earth. It then tracked down and absorbed into itself the lost souls of the Sylvans and Ancients. From Aragmoth, the second Aster was recreated within Earth, and the Sylvans, Ancients and Eminor were later reborn onto it.

Asil — The female Fay twin born to Asteria and Daath on the first Aster. She was an airy spirit who could command all six elements. Aragmoth releases her onto the new Aster without her Sylvan energy in her body, making her more of a physical creature. She is killed by Moon before the end of the Last War and then later reincarnated as Sybl.

Aster — A spiritual and physical world existing inside Earth by means of a Great Dragon known as Aragmoth.

Asteria — While most Sylvan on the first Aster were born as twins, Asteria was born as a Sylph — a treasured rarity that was able to exist by itself without a twin. The spirit of aeri energy was chosen as the leader of the first Aster by the Sylvan kind. Aster was also named after her. Her Bond would later be Daath.

Atrum — A black, tower-like castle, on the center of the Suzerain Continent. It serves as the base of the estus Aur, the death energy from the Great Dragon. It provides a heavier light accompanied by rain and haze and it amplifies negative emotions. It was ruled by Vanir, then later Kas for a short time. Kenshe presently reigns as Atrum Lord.

Atrum City — The city surrounding the Atrum. While it was heavily industrialized from relations with the Falls, it has decayed back to its previous dark-ages state over the last ten years.

Aur — Concentrated estus or aeri energy, usually from the Soph Aur of Toria or the estus Aur of the Atrum. They lighten and darken most of the atmosphere of Aster when they rise individually.

Awls — A creature or shifter possessed by a Sentry who has chosen to 'fall' to Aster and live out their existence. They are natural fortune tellers who can read the Animus Threads connected to one's Fate. Dangerous if angered or insulted, Awls can utilize Thread to their needs, but cannot alter the Threads of gold. Most prefer to live quiet, solitary lives, which also helps them in avoiding Aragmoth's wrath. Considered immortal, dark angels and demons by many. They hide in their human-like appearances that are merely an illusion over their true form, which resembles a dark, winged demon when it touches the Animus Threads of Aster.

Ayame — A female phelan shifter.

Berion — A former town of phelan on the Torian Continent that was not controlled by the Atrum. Jasper and his Bond, Ishtar, were its leaders. Named after Master Berion who is Jasper's father. It is completely destroyed by the Deathmare.

Bond — Another word for mate.

Cael/Caelestis — The Asterian words for god/goddess.

Caller — An ayame capable of creating a Nova which is a powerful song that affects Animus Thread. Ayame are the leaders of their Packs for this reason, as their mastery over the Thread allows them to control their Packs and avoid conflict where possible. In battle, it is often the most powerful ayame Caller who determines the victorious

Pack. Similar rules apply to daoran Novaists, with the exception being that they are all connected to the High Priestess as assistants, instead of being individual leaders like female phelan shifters.

Casus Beli Canyon — Territory of the plumas. Created by Nephena when she hurled Livry across its field in anger of his failure.

Cecil — A 42 year old dragoon, and first born son of Tynar and Trista. His blood falls under the Line of Moon. A mild-hearted dragoon once, Cecil became bitter over the years because of his born blindness, combined with the pressure put on his family by Yri's influences in Toria. His Bond is Rose.

Celia — Gwa's human mother, and a scientist from Earth who once worked for the Falls. She later falls in love with Mersael, but she flees when he tries to kill her and his son, Gwa.

Chimeras — Also known as 'Outcasts.' Soulless and animal-like descendants of Nephena. Chimera are usually a combination of two or more animals. Many have allowed their bodies to be possessed by the Sentry, giving them souls and a human-like form in becoming an Awl.

Cirrus — 38 year old son of Alexia and Simera. Long, straight blond hair and light blue eyes. Born in an abnormal manner as a white dragon, he killed his mother during childbirth. He grew up for thirteen years afterwards incapable of unsomning into his human-like form. His 'human' half is freed shortly after he meets Serena. Later on he discovers that he's actually an Awl similar to his mother.

Custos — Monk-like guardians of the Sanctus. A rank that requires five years of training in both spiritual and martial Arts. They were formed by the late ayame, High Priestess Kira. They include the phelan, humans and some chimeras in their ranks. Their Laws are based off of the teachings of the first Aster that revolve around peace and harmony with both Ancients, Sylvan and Eminor alike. Both females and males may become Custos and those who have talent often go on to become Priests, Callers or Masters. They are forbidden from taking a Bond while serving as a Custos.

Daath — A demon from Earth and formerly one of the 'Four Generals' or 'Four Horsemen' who existed before the Great Flood. He fled to the first Aster to escape enslavement by Hino. Asteria takes him and his army in as refugees, unaware of the consequences it would later bring to her world. She also gives him a soul. Their children are the first Fay of light and darkness; Asil and Erebus.

Damek — Asteria granted Daath a soul during his time on the first Aster, and he later falls in love with her and takes on the new name, Damek. When he was destroyed from the attack of the Dragon Moon, one of his bones is later discovered on Earth by one of Nephena's children and brought to the new Aster. Daath is later fashioned back to life by Tenu and Asil and reconnected with his soul, becoming Damek once again. He disappears after the Last War and is later reborn as Nafury. Daath rejoins with Nafury during his Trial of Somn and the Aeger leads Nafury to his death two years later. Sybl later frees him from Daath's control when he returns possessed by the demon, at the cost of her life.

Daoran — A female Sylvan or female human capable of taking the form of their dragon somn.

Derel — Cecil's younger brother. Second son born of Trista and Tynar.

Dragoon — A male Sylvan or male human capable of taking the form of a dragon.

Dreamwalking — Leaving the body to move about with one's psi through the spiritual plane. This is dangerous as it leaves the soul and spirit vulnerable to more malicious spirits. Those with a strong command over spiritual Thread can manipulate objects and even people.

Efereal Mountains — The snowy home of the chimera Tribes that are led by Xirel.

Elders — The voted council of dragoons and daorans, who assist in upholding their Laws and decisions effecting Toria and the Dragon Caverns.

Eminor — A dark spirit consisting mostly of estus energy. In the days of the first Aster, they were called 'Nightmare Eaters' as they fed off of the negative emotions and nightmares that were unneeded by the Sylvan race. Some chose to become the somns of the reborn Sylvan souls, while many still roam the world as the True.

Erebus — The male Fay twin born to Asteria and Daath on the first Aster. He was an airy spirit who could command all six elements. He was destroyed by the Dragon Moon on the first Aster. Asil wove his life Threads to Aragmoth so he could continue to be able to exist in a partial state of undeath on the second Aster. He dies when the Sylvan City is destroyed. His current reincarnation is Kas, whose soul energy is still bound to Aragmoth.

Estus — A dark, heavy energy most easily channeled through Animus Thread and manipulated through darker emotions such as sadness, hate, anger and jealousy.

Exoir — Griffin shifter, father to Mersael and grandfather to Gwa. He expands the technology of the Falls over Aster using his technical genius. He has an uncommon snowy leopard hide on his cat half as a griffin. Exoir was once Avian, the General of Pestilence.

Fay — A creature that is able to balance both aeri and estus energy within themselves and at the same time.

Feharin Army — The Sylvan's army.

Festra — A curved, staff-like weapon that holds a blade within its ends. Though effective in combat, the original purpose of the festra was to control and cut

Threads, killing or enslaving enemy names to it. Only Asteria, Asil, Damek and Erebus can fully wield this weapon, as most of the names bound to it will only answer to them. The Threads were broken and its slaves freed when the weapon was transported through the Soph Aur by Luna.

Four Generals — On Earth, they were called the Four Horsemen; Pestilence, War, Famine and Death. When they left Earth to escape to the first Aster, they became Avian, Reol, Gei and Daath. They have souls that were given to them by Asteria and are no longer controllable by Hino. They are acknowledged as the highest and most powerful level of Sentry, Iynx, and Awls.

Gate — A machine that artificially stabilizes a Rift and passage to the Keol, another Gate, or Earth with estus energy. The mer created the first Gate.

Gei — Formerly known as the General of Famine, he was the last true form of an Iynx spirit on Aster who protected the Sanctus. Only Kira is said to have ever seen his human-like form. In an attempt to prevent Kira from falling in love with him, he strips his wings from his back and his ability to hide his form with a human-like illusion weave is lost as a result.

Gloria — A fiery redhead, green-eyed human. Former Dockmistress of the Atrum's Harbor on the Suzerain Continent. She used to oversee all the ships coming and going from the Harbor and trading relations between the

Torian Continent. Before coming to Aster, she was a singer. She was the former owner of the GLORIA.

Griffin — Half cat, half bird chimeras. They have the head, wings, tail and front legs of a bird, and the rest of their bodies is that of a large cat. When separated from their hosts, they resemble a ribbon of electricity. They believe they are the only god-chosen (Hino) creatures worthy of commanding over Aster. They are plagued by diseases and disabilities that force their Tech and medical sciences forward out of necessity. Their home was the Falls, a Tech-rich city built in the dormant crater of a volcano that was once considered impenetrable. The Falls was ruled by Exoir. Now it exists only as empty ruins.

Gwa — 24 years old, dusty red and white hair, brown eyes. He is a griffin shifter. His mother, Celia, is a human scientist from Earth and his father is the griffin shifter, Mersael, who abandoned them for the sake of his position. Gwa was a close friend of Kas and a Custos.

Harbor — The Harbor is controlled mostly by the Atrum, but is occupied by independent businesses and ship owners as well.

High Guard — Dragoons who serve in the army for Toria. It is required that they serve for at least five years before they are allowed to take a Bond for themselves and have a family. These Laws are based on the Texts of the Sylvan Order, which required military service and an acceptable status prior to marriage, thus ensuring the skill and strength to raise and protect a family. Usually one is initiated into the military after surviving their Trial of Somn that defines one as an adult with the equivalent strength.

Hino — God of thunder and lightning and guardian of the skies of Earth. Believed to be the One Cael of Earth and the leader of the Sentry. Though speculation has also suggested that he is a consciousness consisting of many consciouses.

Iynx — Sentry who once roamed Aster in their true forms, who were cut free from Hino's control by Asil. On Earth their bodies are usually winged and insect-like, but their forms are distorted by Aster's Animus Threads and expanded, making them look more 'fuzzy' and cat-like. All Iynx can manipulate Thread to give them the illusion of a human-like appearance or whatever appearance they learn. Gei is the last known Iynx to exist on Aster in his true form, as other Iynx have much shorter life expectancies.

Jru — Former Armsman and Custos of the Sanctus. A martial and spiritual Arts teacher who served and tutored Kas as his own, never forgetting the tragedy of what happened to Kira as she trained him as one of her first Custos. His peaceful Tribe that consisted mostly of phelan shifters were taken in by the Sanctus when it was annihilated by Simera's High Guard when he was still a child. His father is believed to still be alive, but he went into exile to carry the sins with him of failing to protect Jru's ayame mother who was killed in the attack.

Kas — 28 years old and son of Kira and Vanir. The youngest Priest ever anointed on the Suzerain or Torian Continents. He fears the darker force of Erebus' spirit within him and often chooses to be alone so he can better control his emotions. His spiritual and military prowess is well beyond his years. He fades into Aragmoth before Sybl's death.

Kenshe — 24 years old and one of Kas' best friends and a former Custos. Dark auburn hair and grey eyes. He is a grizzled brown in his phelan form. Son of Hain and Kayla. Born as a True phelan, he discovers his soul and ability to unsomn later when he is four. But his mother never accepts him as her own despite it. After Kas dies, he is elected as the new Atrum Lord.

Keol — Also called the 'Blood Tears' of Aragmoth. The phelan often use this fiery tempest of a desert and lava plane to travel, as the cold estus energy of their being keeps them from igniting or being burned. Phelan blood can open a Rift in and out of this plane, as well as creatures consisting of mostly estus energy.

Kira — Ayame founder and the first High Priestess of the Sanctus. Once the best Caller of the Atrum, she chose to leave the corruption that Vanir ruled it by. She is killed by Vanir by accident when she steps between what would have been a lethal strike to Master Gei. Her son is Kas.

Kyrie — A deer-like creature that is muscularly built for harder labours like a workhorse and is often captured and trained to be put to use as such. Individually, they are timid and controllable but become dangerous and difficult when within a herd. Their single, thick horn is curved down to their backs. Their feet are cloven like a goat's and their tail is like that of a lion, giving them the nickname of 'unicorns' by humans from Earth. They can be anywhere from white to black, and countless shades of brown in between.

Loki — 33 years old and son of Crystal and Estar. Thin, light green hair to shoulders and orange eyes. His frailer physique has green, star-like markings over his eyes. His brother was Lintrance and his half-sister is Kayla. He has mixed feelings for Sybl, mostly as the memory of his mother's death and unborn sister still haunts him. Sybl helped fill the gap in his heart left by their loss. He dies after the collapse of Mer City, but returns as an Awl.

Mei — A connection of Animus Threads between two individuals, usually Bonds, that allows for greater protection by eliminating the disadvantage of using the slower-conducting spiritual Animus. Its literal meaning is 'shield.' Its meaning is now a more general one that includes the glyph-like silver Threads on both sexes. The individuals share each other emotions and thoughts and it is useful for different species in different ways and circumstances, particularly dangerous ones. It is an unbreakable connection between Bonds, and often when one mate dies, the other shortly follows.

Mer/Mermaids — Descendants of Tenu and humans, they once dwelled in the depths of the Eternal Waters, where the estus energy they need to survive is the strongest. They take mentally and physically ill extremely easily and weaken when near aeri energy for too long. There are no mermaids known to still be alive.

Mersael — Griffin shifter and son of Exoir. Long straight white hair, yellow eyes. Former husband to Celia and father of Gwa. He was engineered by Exoir as a perfect child and was born without a mother, which many blame his cold, uncaring nature for.

Moon — The dark, estus essence of the Dragon Moon and Eminor of sacrifice. Given as a gift to Asil from Nephena, he is raised by Asil as the avatar of Aragmoth's will. When he accidentally kills Asil after he finds his soul, his being is split back into two in his fight against the Phoenix that ends the Last War. He later becomes Cirrus' somn for a while, and his sacrifice contains and helps destroy Daath when the demon is separated from Nafury.

Nafury — 25 year old former Prince of Toria. Wavy brown hair and sapphire blue eyes. Born to Serena as the purposeful reincarnation of Damek. Simera adopted him as his own son out of his love for Serena. He is born with Sybl in Mer City and is separated from her when she is immediately sent to Earth.

Nephena — Chimera Mother of the second Aster. She has a lion's body and head, a goat's head on her shoulder, and a snake for a tail. All three heads have separate minds. Fashioned to life by Aragmoth from many animals of Earth. She cannot give her children souls, making her dependent on Asil.

Outcast — Another word for chimeras.

Pack — A phelan Pack has two to a dozen members. Although several males answer to one female, it is only the Alpha who is her mate, and he alone is responsible for using the ayame's psi and foresight to issue orders to the Pack. This is not a guaranteed position, and if he becomes incapable of being the Alpha, he is usually disposed of by a challenge from the next most powerful in the Pack. If at any point the ayame dies due to a failure on her Pack's part, the Pack usually splits off and its members are either driven out or have the utmost difficulty being accepted by another ayame.

Phelan — Large, wolf-like creatures with many cat-like features. They use their own blood to travel in and out of the Keol and to sync with their Pack. Females are called ayame and are more slender-featured and cat-like, though they tend to be of a dark black in fur and hair as opposed to the males who can be seen as lighter grays, browns and black. Most have red eyes, though they cannot see the color red and see the color of the other's intentions, instead. Any phelan referred to as 'True' exist without a human-like form and soul, and are still a spirit. On the first Aster, they were a type of 'Nightmare Eater' resembling wolves that came from Earth to escape their enslavement to Hino. They were later refashioned into their own species on the second Aster by Damek.

Phoenix — Somn of Solar, the Phoenix was a massive, winged serpent surrounded by a constant fire. Once a smaller serpent, it expanded considerably in its battle against Moon, and even more so for the last three hundred years on Earth under its sun. Its sickening fire of radiation burns Animus Threads and it is lethal when exposed to creatures of Aster for too long. The Falls helps Rose, Solar's reincarnation, to venture to Earth where she regains her Phoenix.

Pluma — The Asterian word for winged cats. When angered, they are a formable enemy that unleash their full extent in swarms. Regals are the larger male plumas.

Prisca — A 19 year old ayame. Daughter of Tank. Sybl unknowingly meets her in the Harbor shortly after arriving on the Suzerain Continent for the first time. She is currently Kenshe's High Caller.

Psi — Also known as telepathy. It is limited by distance which can be extended by a strong Caller, Novaist, Mei, or an Awl. Gold also amplifies psi tremendously.

Regal — Male plumas born larger with colourful

wings to serve as frontline defenders and watchers. Their bodies resemble that of a lion's and their impressive wingspans are coloured and printed like that of a peacock's. A full grown Regal can be as massive as a dragon mostly by bulk. They can fold their feathers together in such a way to make them into knives, and propel them like darts at their adversaries. A swarm of them is an unstoppable storm of sharp feathers, claws, teeth and sheer weight. Their wings and bodies hold high concentrations of aeri energy, allowing them to fly with ease, but it makes them vulnerable to fire and the Keol. They can be found on the Casus Beli fields with their wings folded tightly together and raised like lightning poles to the sky.

Rift — A 'tear' in the spiritual Thread of Aragmoth that serves as a passage into the Keol. A deep enough Rift can reach as far as Earth. Phelan and creatures consisting of mostly estus energy can create Rifts.

Rose — 40 years old and Cecil's Bond who was adopted by Ishtar and Jasper. Short red hair, green eyes. She has a natural ability to see the future as Solar's reincarnation. Yri goes out of her way to push her from Cecil's life, fearing that Rose's talent surpasses her own. She is later manipulated by Mersael and the Falls, crafting her into a decimating weapon to their cause after she heads to Earth through the Gate at the town of Berion. There she is reunited with her somn, the Phoenix.

When she attacks the Sanctus and destroys it, Gei springs a trap on her and separates her soul from the fiery spirit. He returns Rose to Cecil.

Sanctus — Founded by the ayame Kira, this former temple of peace was built on the Sylvan Laws of the first Aster. Safe haven and neutral sanctuary to all religions and races alike. Its guardians were the Custos who can be almost any kind of shifter. It is completely destroyed by the Phoenix.

Sano — Another word for a Master over aeri energy in the Arts of Healing.

Sentry — Servants of the god Hino, they reside mostly on Earth. Visible only by a strong spiritual sense, they aggressively protect Earth and its humans from Asterians by killing any eminor or Ancients who venture near them. They are massive, insect-like creatures.

Serena — Sybl's and Nafury's human mother, who went through a Gate to find her best friend, Alexia. Kira later finds her and she spends some time at the Sanctus, where she befriends her. She later gets taken by Simera and falls in love with him. She dies after Simera leaves for Earth to find her daughter who was taken from her after being born.

Sial — A unicorn given to Asteria from Damek as a wedding present. His horn is the festra that had the names of all 3000 Eminor loyal to Damek Threaded to it. Sial is reincarnated through Nephena at the end of the Last War, after Damek strikes the Chimera Mother with the festra. The festra returns to Sial as his horn, and he escapes with it. He presently follows Nafury around as the fabled 'Deathmare.'

Simera — Former King of Toria and the dragons. His Sylvan form is that of long, wavy mauve hair and light blue eyes. Simera's age is unknown, but few question his bloodline that supposedly leads directly back to Moon, as his physical and spiritual strength is unmatched. Rumor says that he is another illegitimate son of Svarog, while others claim he is the son of a True. He becomes King by his unmatched power when the dragons take Toria from the chimeras after the Last War, killing those who challenge him for leadership. He is never seen again after he goes to Earth to find Sybl.

Solar — The first shifter daughter from Nephena. She holds a bitter jealously towards Asil and tries to take the Sylvan City from the Fay behind her back. Her reincarnation is Rose and her somn is the Phoenix.

Somn/Somnus/Shifter — Somns are the spirit form that a soul can become in the physical. Named such as the soul is said to rest while the spirit is physically materialized by its host's energy. The soul slows in aging while somned, much like a deep sleep, which is why many shifters can live a hundred years or more. Shifters never actually sleep, as their souls are always conscious and when they aren't, then the animalistic nature of the somn takes over and they go berserk.

Suzerain Continent — The second Continent of the three that were split apart at the end of the Last War by Aragmoth's wrath.

Svarog — The first fire dragoon born of Nephena and Moon. He had black hair with orange eyes and was a black dragon. A natural blacksmith.

Sybl — A 25 year old woman from Earth, who was sent into foster care when she was 13 after her attempted suicide. Long wavy brown hair, dark blue eyes. As the reincarnation of Asil, she remembers who she was in her past life. The Sylvan Aur exists within her. She dies exorcising Daath from Nafury.

Sylvan — Similar to humans, they were the inhabitants of the first Aster. They were originally spirits in servitude to Hino, until one was discovered amongst them who could give them souls. When their soul-giver was destroyed by Hino, the Sylvan fled Earth to a star, where they made a habitable planet of it. Many Ancients followed them. When their soul-giver was reborn to them as the Sylph Asteria, they became a prosperous, powerful and happy race up until the planet's destruction by the Dragon Moon.

Sylvan Aur — The blue light that is the result of estus and aeri energy being together in balance, that is also an equilibrium for the estus and aeri Aurs on Aster. Fay are the only creatures known to be able to safely create this energy without explosive consequences. The Sylvan Aur was destroyed with the Sylvan City and restored after Daath's defeat.

Sylvan City — Also known as the Golden City, where Sylvans, Ancients and Eminor could co-exist in peace 300 years ago. The Last War eventually led to the city's destruction, when the Phoenix and Moon fought it out in the Sylvan Aur, causing an explosion that decimated the city in a rain of fire.

Toria — A white castle that rises around the Ain Soph Aur and spirals outwards into the Sylvan Woods. It is the main holding and home to the dragons. Its Aur rises and falls every twelve hours. Its walls glow a warmth of white light even when the Aur is down, making the tower visible at night as well as day. It is surrounded by four waterfalls that are fed by the Lunar Waters, that rise at its sides, keeping the castle constantly surrounded by mists and rainbows.

Trial of Somn — Different for phelan and dragons, the Trial is an initiation into adulthood to unite with one's Ancient or eminor and be able to host the spirit from their body. For phelan, this Trial includes crossing the Ice Fields and defeating a snow serpent, then offering it as a sacrifice to their somn as proof of their strength. If successful, the phelan returns with a somn and are then capable of taking the form of a phelan. Those who fail are usually killed. The Trial must be done alone.

For dragons, their Trial includes swimming to the deepest reaches of the Eternal Waters and finding their shadow, then pulling it forth to take the dragon form for themselves. One must have the strength to survive the pressure and the enemies who exist underwater. Failing can lead to drowning or being eaten by a larger sea creature, though dragon Trials are usually done as a small group so dying doesn't happen often.

True phelan — The Eminor of the first Aster and a type of Nightmare Eater, originating from Earth and once bound by their names to the festra. They once served as slaves to the Sentry and were more demon-like. Damek later refashions them into their own wolf-like species. They are now phelan spirits without a soul.

Unicorn — See kyrie.

Vanir — Long black straight hair, red eyes. The reigning phelan shifter Atrum Lord of the Suzerain Continent. He claimed the throne 250 years ago, just fifty years after the Last War. His age is well past that of most mortals and his power and ability to manipulate those to his will are unsurpassed. His parents are unknown. He dies from old age before Sybl's death.

Xirel — 300+ year old Tribe leader of the chimeras in the Efereal Mountains. He became an Awl like many of his kind. He resembles a large, silver deer with purple eyes when somned, and long white hair and purple eyes in his human-like appearance.

ABOUT THE AUTHOR

S.J. Wist is a fantasy author, reviewer, and an artist on the side. Addicted to books, blogs, chocolate mint ice cream, and all things creative. She lives in Toronto, Canada.

S.J. Wist

Dragon Aster

Trilogy

S.J. WIST

WHISPERING STONE